THE BLUE STAR

Also by Tony Earley

Jim the Boy
Here We Are in Paradise
Somehow Form a Family

THE BLUE STAR

A NOVEL

TONY EARLEY

LITTLE, BROWN AND COMPANY

New York   Boston   London

Little, Brown and Company
Hachette Book Group USA
237 Park Avenue, New York, NY 10017
Visit our Web site at www.HachetteBookGroupUSA.com

First Edition: March 2008

The characters and events in this book are fictitious. Any similarity to real
persons, living or dead, is coincidental and not intended by the author.

Library of Congress Cataloging-in-Publication Data

Earley, Tony.
   The blue star : a novel / Tony Earley. — 1st ed.
      p. cm.
   ISBN-13: 978-0-316-19907-0
   ISBN-10: 0-316-19907-9
   1. Teenage boys — Fiction.   2. Nineteen forties — Fiction.   I. Title.
   PS3555.A685B56 2008
   813'.54 — dc22   2007009921

10   9   8   7   6   5   4   3   2   1

RRD-IN

PRINTED IN THE UNITED STATES OF AMERICA

For
The girls who live in the blue house

I got a pig home in the pen
And corn to feed him on
All I need is a pretty little girl
To feed him when I'm gone

Arthur Smith,
"Pig in a Pen"

In memory of
Gordon Kato
1961–2006

CONTENTS

CONTENTS

Book III: Unexpected News

Book IV: The Blue Star

Prologue

Lynn's Mountain, NC
Dear Zeno,

It is a cold day up here, and though a few trees are start-ing to bud and a few brave wildflowers are coming up in the sunny places, I'm afraid it will never be spring again. There is still snow on the other side of the hollow and I don't think it will ever melt. I still feel awful about the fight we had last Sunday when you rode all the way up here on your white mule in the mud just to see me and you got so cold, and I wish that I felt different from what I said then but I still don't. I will never understand as long as I live why you do not want to do your duty and join up for the fight with our boys "over there." Boys from NC and this county are being blowed up and shot in the head by the Germans, even boys from this mountain, like poor Alfred Summey. You even rode by his house on that handsome white mule you're so proud of and saw that awful wreath on the door. Zeno, I thought I loved you with all my heart forever but maybe I don't anymore if I ever did, because I don't really know who you are. All the other boys I know have either been drafted already or have joined up or are getting ready to. Even Al-fred Summey's little brother William is raring to go fight the Huns and he is only twelve years old and he is afraid the war will be over before he can get to France and make up for his brother who was killed, and he just breaks my heart. Don't you feel awful, Zeno, when everybody else is doing their part and you don't do yours? If there was a dam about to bust and wash everybody's house away and you saw all your *friends working trying to fix it, would you ride on by on that big mule and just tip your hat howdy or would you get down and help? Zeno, I don't think I can be married to a man who would just ride by that dam and let everybody else's house get washed away, especially when there are twelve-year-old boys begging to help dig. I don't know how you can live with yourself in these awful times and I don't know how you expect me to live with you either, the way things are. I intend to marry a man I can be proud of, and right now I just don't think I can be proud of you because of the decisions you have made. Everybody up here is already calling you a "shirker" and worse and they say your daddy paid and fixed it so your number wouldn't come up, and how do you think that makes me feel? Is riding up here pretty as you please when you know everybody you pass on the road hates you the only brave thing you can do? (I have heard people say that if you keep coming up in here anymore, somebody is bound to shoot you!) This is the hardest thing I've ever had to say in my life but it is the truth. If you had joined the army when everybody else did, I would have waited on you until the end of the earth, but I can't wait on you anymore. When I hear about somebody I can trust going down your way, I will send the ring with them. I cannot keep it anymore or wear it on my finger. I am very sorry and I hope that someday you will be able to see that this is right and forgive me in your heart.*

Love always,
Nancy

November 21, 1941

Dear Jim
    Hey old buddy I bet you never expected to hear from me did you? Have you started getting ready for baseball season yet? It'll be here before you know it so you better get in shape! Now that I'm gone I guess shortstop is all yours. You ought to be able to handle it after watching "the master" play it for three years straight. Ha!
    I just got stationed on the USS California I guess you heard. It is the best ship in the navy. Where else would you expect me to be? Ha! You would not believe how beautiful Hawaii is. Is it cold there yet? Not here boy. I would bring a palm tree and the ocean home with me if I could. The food on the ship is "OK."
    Hey Jim a little "birdy" tells me that you've been sniffing around Chrissie Steppe. As you know she's my "girl" but maybe you just forgot. Don't forget that I'm not dead I'm just in the navy! They're not the same thing! Ha! Anyway the last thing you want to do is make a sailor mad. Don't forget to cover the old "sack" like I taught you once the season starts!

Your friend,
Arthur Bucklaw Jr. USN

BOOK I

Indian Summer

At the Top

BECAUSE THEY were seniors and had earned the right, Jim and his buddies stood on the small landing at the top of the school steps, squarely in front of the red double doors. Every student entering the building, boy or girl, had to go around them to get inside. The boys pretended not to notice that they were in everyone else's way, and moved aside only when a teacher climbed the stairs. They had ruled Aliceville School for less than a month but now held this high ground more or less comfortably. The first few days of school, Jim had halfway expected some older boys to come along and tell them to get lost, but during the preceding three weeks, he had gradually come to appreciate that there were no older boys. He and his friends were *it*.

The school overlooked the town from atop a steep hill. Jim tilted his face slightly into the clear sunlight and tenderly considered the world below him. At the foot of the hill the houses and barns and sheds of Aliceville lay scattered around the town's small tangle of streets. Near the center of town the uncles' three tall houses stood shoulder to shoulder. (Jim lived with his mother and her oldest brother, Uncle Zeno, in the middle house. Uncle Coran and Uncle Al, who were twins, lived on either side.) Beyond the town itself, across the railroad track, the uncles' corn and cotton crops filled the sandy bottoms all the way to their arable edges; beyond the fields the neatly tended rows unraveled into the thick gnarl of woods through which the river snaked. The corn, still richly green, stood taller than any man, and the dark cotton rows were speckled with dots of bright, emerging white. West of town the engine smoke of an approaching train climbed into the sky.

Jim could not see Uncle Zeno or Uncle Al in the fields, nor Uncle Coran in the store, but he knew they were there, the same way he knew that when the time came to pick cotton they would not ask him to skip school to help. Just as he wondered what his mother was doing, Mama came out the front door of Uncle Zeno's house with a bucket and dipper and began watering the chrysanthemums blooming in the pots on the porch steps. She glanced at the orange bus from Lynn's Mountain as it turned off the state highway and ground its way up the pitched drive. Jim was glad she didn't look all the way up the hill toward the school. Had she seen him and waved, he not only would have been embarrassed, but he would also have been tempted to weep with some mysterious, nostalgic joy. The warm sunlight on his face seemed to remind him of something — but he couldn't explain what — and some vague but pleasant longing filled his chest. Already he could sense the end of these good days rapidly approaching, like a mail train filled with unexpected news.

"Hey, Jim," Buster Burnette said, "there's your mama."

Dennis Deane squinted as he looked down the hill. "What's she doing?"

"Daggum, Dennis Deane," Jim said. "You can't see a lick, can you?"

"I don't need to see," Dennis Deane said. "I've got an extra eyeball."

Everybody grinned, but nobody said anything. They all knew better.

Dennis Deane batted his eyes innocently. "Ain't you going to ask me where it is?"

Jim shook his head. "Ain't no way."

"Cowards," Dennis Deane sniffed. "The whole bunch of you." He cleared his throat. "Now, where was I?"

"The secrets of women," said Larry Lawter.

"Oh, yeah. Like I said, I know the secrets of women. I can make any female I want to fall in love with me."

"Bull," Buster said.

"I'm telling you," Dennis Deane said. "I'm the Large Possum. The King of the Squirrels."

"You're a nut is what you are," said Jim.

"The Head Nut," Dennis Deane said. "Twice as much for a nickel. Try me just once and you'll know why."

The bus grumbled to a stop at the bottom of the steps. The doors swung open and the students from Lynn's Mountain climbed off and curled around the front of the bus. In the distance the train announced itself at the state highway crossing with a long blast from its whistle. Jim wondered about the train because it was not one that was regularly scheduled. Like everyone else who lived in Aliceville, Jim knew the timetables of the trains and noted when they passed, even in his sleep.

"Prove it," Larry said. "What you said about women." He jerked his head toward the bus. "How about one of these mountain girls?"

"How about her?" Buster said, nodding at a freshman girl with green, shrewd-looking eyes who came around the front of the bus with her books clutched closely to her chest. A pack of third- and fourth-grade boys chattered by her and up the steps into the building. The girl did not look at the seniors on the landing, but Jim could tell she knew they were there.

Dennis Deane squinted again. "Who is it?" he asked. "What's her name?"

"Ellie," Buster said. "Ellie something."

"Okay," Dennis Deane said. "Ellie something. Watch and learn, boys."

When the girl reached the landing, Dennis Deane said, "Hey, Ellie Something." When she looked up, he closed his eyes and contorted his face into an enormous pucker. "Kiss me," he said.

Jim winced when he saw the stricken look on Ellie's face and stepped out of the way to aid her escape. She jerked open one of the doors and ran inside.

"You shouldn't have done that, Dennis Deane," he said, although, despite his better judgment, he laughed along with everybody else.

"I knew it wouldn't work," Buster said.

"Of course it worked," said Dennis Deane. "Ellie Something is now in love with me, although, bless her little heart, she would never, ever admit it. She's just too shy."

Otis Shehan and Horace Gentine climbed the steps and joined the group. The mountain boys were also seniors. "Howdy, men," Horace said. "How's it hanging?"

"Try it on her," Larry said, nodding toward Christine Steppe.

No, don't, Jim thought, but he didn't say anything. As far as Jim was concerned, watching Chrissie Steppe climb the stairway was the best part of the day. And because this information seemed valuable to him in some way he could not name, he had never told the other guys.

"Try what on her?" Otis asked. "I wouldn't try anything on her. That's Bucky Bucklaw's girl."

"I don't care if it's Franklin D. Roosevelt's girl," Dennis Deane said. "Hey. Chrissie Steppe. Kiss me." He squeezed his eyes shut and puckered up.

Chrissie stopped and her large, dark eyes blinked

slowly as she considered Dennis Deane. Her black hair reached almost to her waist. She shifted her books to her left arm.

Jim noticed that her right hand was balled into a dangerous-looking fist. "Hey, whoa," he said, stepping in front of her. "Don't hit him."

Dennis Deane flinched. "Hit me?" he said, without opening his eyes. "Is somebody about to hit me?"

Chrissie's shoulders rose and fell with her breathing. "I'm about to beat you all over this schoolyard, you little worm," she said. "I will not be talked to that way."

Dennis Deane covered his head with his arms and whimpered, "Don't hurt me, you big, strong, she-girl."

"He didn't mean anything by it," said Jim. "He's just a little, well, insane, is what he is."

"I've got an extra eyeball," Dennis Deane said. "Do you want me to show it to you?"

Chrissie turned away from Dennis Deane and stared levelly at Jim with what he took to be an expression of slight disappointment. "Are you his friend?" she asked.

"Sort of, I guess," he said. "More like his guardian. Something like that."

Jim caught a slight whiff of vanilla and wished she would step even closer. He felt himself beginning to smile and thought, wildly, *We're almost close enough to kiss.*

Chrissie did not smile back, but she opened her fist. "Well. You tell your little friend that I will not stand for *any*one talking to me like that. Ever. You tell him that if he talks to me that way again, I will beat him like a borrowed mule."

"Hee-*haw*," Dennis Deane said from behind Jim.

"Dennis Deane," Jim warned over his shoulder. "Shut *up*."

"I mean it, Jim Glass," Chrissie said.

"I know you do," said Jim.

"You tell him."

"I will."

Chrissie nodded once, turned on her heel, and pulled open the door. Then she was gone. Nobody laughed, although Jim wanted to. He felt wonderfully, inexplicably happy.

Dennis Deane stepped out from behind Jim and made a show of adjusting his shirt collar. He blew into his palm, checking his breath.

"Well," he said. "She loves me. Write it down in the big book, boys. Write it down."

"She was going to knock you out," Larry said.

"I should have let her hit you," Jim said.

"Don't mess around with that girl," said Otis. "I'm serious. If she doesn't beat your ass, then Bucky will when he gets home on leave."

"Bucky Bucklaw," Dennis Deane scoffed. "How am I supposed to be afraid of somebody with a name that stupid?"

Larry pointed down the hill at the long passenger train drawing a thick silver line through town. "Hey, look at that," he said.

The windows of the coaches were open, and men in uniforms, their shirtsleeves rolled up, were hanging out most of them. Soldiers. A whole trainload of them. Jim wondered what they saw when they looked at Aliceville, if anything would make an impression worth remembering; he wondered where they were going.

"Troop train," he said.

"What?" Dennis Deane said. "Has the train got soldiers on it?"

The bell rang. The boys picked up their books.

"You're blind as a mole," Jim said.

"I don't need to see," said Dennis Deane. "I've got an extra eyeball."

A History Lesson

*A*t the start of fifth period Jim was already seated in history class when Chrissie Steppe walked through the door. She sat every day at the desk immediately in front of his. This was another, although brand-new, reason that Jim thought history his favorite subject. As he watched her make her way across the room, Jim slid his desk forward until it bumped against the back of Chrissie's chair. He opened his history book without looking at the page and pushed it forward until it, too, touched the back of her chair. He opened his mouth to say something as she approached, but she didn't look at him; he closed his mouth without ever knowing what it was he would have said.

When Chrissie sat down, she leaned forward, slid both hands beneath her hair at the base of her neck and flipped it away from her body over the top rung of her chair, almost hitting Jim in the face, so that she would not lean back against it. It spilled onto his open book just as he had hoped it would. He sat and gaped.

Chrissie's hair almost obscured the pages about the blockade of Wilmington during the Civil War.

Miss Brown — who had taught Mama and all three of the uncles and, so far as Jim knew, Moses and Aaron — shuffled into class before the bell rang and began calling the roll. She was tall and stooped and thin as a broom handle. She never waited for the bell to ring before calling the roll, no matter how often the students complained. She had spent most of her career teaching in two- and three-room schoolhouses without electricity and apparently either did not understand what the bell was for or simply refused to acknowledge its existence. When she reached Jim's name, he said, "Present," in a loud voice. He liked to say *present* instead of *here* because it aggravated his friends, particularly Dennis Deane, who said it was a teacher's-pet kind of thing to say.

The subject that day was the early European exploration of America, but Jim paid only sporadic attention. He studied instead, with a scholar's single-minded intensity, the way the light reflected off Chrissie's black hair. The day before, Jim had noticed that when the sun hit it just right, it sparkled with the deep colors of a prism hanging in the window of a science class. Today he wanted to see if he had imagined it. He studied it so closely that his eyes slipped out of focus and the scale of the room swelled in an instant and became immense around him; he felt suddenly microscopic, a tiny creature swimming in a drop of pond water. At that moment Chrissie's hair seemed to take on an infinite depth; it became a warm, rich space into which it suddenly seemed possible to fall and become lost. Off in the distance somewhere he heard Miss Brown say the word *conquistador*. She always trilled the *r* and added a long *a* sound to the end of the word, a pronunciation that made most of the students snicker. But Jim thought it sounded romantic and filled with adventure, an altogether fitting word for men who sailed across oceans and waded into strange jungles, searching for lost cities of gold. *"Conquistador,"* Jim whispered, adding the long *a*. He leaned forward almost imperceptibly and moved his head slightly in relation to the sunlight falling through the tall windows.

There.

The colors of the spectrum flared in Chrissie's hair with the hopeful radiance of undiscovered stars. Jim sat very still and held his breath, aware that he had entered a magical place where it would not be possible to stay. The colors and lights swirled around him in their private orbits. He was sure that he knew something about Chrissie Steppe that no one else knew, that maybe no one else in the world would ever know. He certainly doubted that Bucky Bucklaw, who was a lunkhead, knew about Chrissie's hair. The moment he thought about Bucky Bucklaw, however, the colors in Chrissie's hair blinked out, and the scale of the room spun back to normal. Jim found himself back in North Carolina, in Aliceville, at his desk in history class, his history book covered with the beautiful hair of a girl he barely knew, who probably didn't like him, anyway. According to Miss Brown, Ponce de León's men staggered through the swamps of Florida until they collapsed, their lungs filled with the mosquitoes they had no choice but to inhale. They never discovered the fountain of youth.

Jim sighed.

He opened his notebook and wrote "ROY G. BIV" in block letters at the top of a clean piece of paper. Then he wrote "RED ORANGE YELLOW GREEN BLUE INDIGO VIOLET." He looked at what he had written and realized it wouldn't be much help in studying for a history test. He forced himself to turn his attention to Miss Brown, who had moved from Ponce de León on to Hernando de Soto. Jim wrote "de Soto" in his notebook.

"We North Carolinians," Miss Brown said, "speak with justifiable pride about Sir Walter Raleigh and the Lost Colony, and about poor Virginia Dare, born on the hostile shores of the New World, never to be heard from again, but what we do not regularly speak of, perhaps because we are of English descent, is the expedition of the great *conquistador* Hernando de Soto into what is now North Carolina in the early fifteen forties, years before our beloved Raleigh was even born. Search in the history book on your desk all you like and you will find no mention of de Soto's expedition into the Tarheel State. Why is that? I do not know, children. Most of the decisions made in Raleigh have always struck me as illogical, if not arcane.

But, had history played out in a slightly different manner, this class today would be conducted entirely in
Spanish. And wouldn't you find that confusing?"

Miss Brown seemed to think this very funny. She
put her hand to her chest and snorted, her face red-
dening. "Oh, my," she said. "*Muy bueno.*"

Jim wrote "#1" and "NC" in his notebook beside
the word "de Soto." This, finally, seemed to be a fact
worth remembering.

"Allow me to tell you a story," Miss Brown continued when she recovered.

Here we go, thought Jim.

"My maternal grandmother grew up not far from
here, near Tryon. Her family owned a small planta-
tion, which, by the way, the male descendants of my
family have managed to squander over the years until
not a shred of it remains in our possession. Not a
shred, children. Be that as it may, my grandmother's
people owned a few slaves, no more than ten, I suppose, at any one time — this was only a small planta-
tion, you see — but they owned a few. One of those
slaves, an old fellow named Big Walker, told my grandmother, when she was just a little girl herself, that,
when *he* was a young man on a neighboring planta-
tion, he had plowed up a steel helmet and a fine
sword. The helmet and sword were, of course, Spanish in provenance, which would prove, incontrovert-
ibly, that de Soto passed not only through western
North Carolina but through *our* part of western North
Carolina. The helmet and sword were, naturally,

turned over by Big Walker to his master, in whose possession they remained until the War Between the States. According to my grandmother, when that gentleman went off to fight for the Confederacy, he reburied that helmet and sword, lest those artifacts be seized by Yankee foragers in his absence. Alas, he did not tell anyone where he had buried these treasures, and he did not return from the war to reclaim them. To my knowledge, they are to this day buried still beneath the soil of Polk County, waiting to be discovered yet again."

Miss Brown sighed theatrically. "To think," she said, "that I knew someone who knew someone who once held in his very hands a sword and helmet worn by a member of de Soto's army."

Jim held his pencil poised above his notebook, his brow furrowed. He wondered if any Spanish artifacts were buried in the uncles' fields but had no idea what to write down. Miss Brown rarely seemed to talk about anything that was actually *in* the history book. After almost a month of classes, he had no idea what she would put on their exams. She had yet to give them even a quiz. Jim decided to read the book, anyway, just in case. He glanced down at the book and wondered what Chrissie's hair smelled like.

"I have often wondered," Miss Brown went on, "how that helmet and sword came to be abandoned by their Spanish owner. For surely nothing could be more important to a soldier in a hostile land than his helmet and sword. Without them he would be defenseless against his enemies. Obviously, some great tragedy must have befallen him. The only plausible answer I can think of to such a perplexing question is that he was slaughtered by the Cherokee, whose ancestral lands the Spanish were at the time claiming for the crown of Spain. Miss Steppe, you are at least partially descended from the Cherokee, are you not?"

Jim saw Chrissie stiffen.

"I don't know," she said.

"Wasn't your father a Cherokee? That's what I have always heard. That would explain your lovely hair."

"I'm not sure. He never said."

In his notebook Jim wrote "INDIAN?"

"Perhaps he was only part Cherokee?" Miss Brown went on.

"Which part?" Dennis Deane asked, to a smattering of coughs and snorts, from across the room.

That's enough, Dennis Deane, Jim thought. He squirmed in his seat, cleared his throat, raised his hand, and asked, "Miss Brown, do you think de Soto and his army might have come through Aliceville?"

"That's an interesting question, Mr. Glass," Miss Brown said. "In the future, please wait until I acknowledge you before speaking."

"Yes, ma'am," Jim said.

"To answer your question, asked rudely though it may have been, I think it's entirely possible that de Soto's army passed through Aliceville, although, of course, it wasn't Aliceville at the time. If it had a name at all, it would have been some Cherokee name we

could never hope to recall. Still, our river passes near
Tryon, where Big Walker discovered the Spanish helmet and sword, and was de Soto following our river
west, which seems to me a likely route, he easily could
have passed this way. Isn't that something to think
about?"

"Yes, ma'am," Jim said.

"Indeed, de Soto himself might have climbed this
very hill to survey the surrounding countryside, for
this is the only vantage point of any elevation nearby.
Perhaps he saw our blue mountains in the distance
and thought that surely there he and his men would
find the cities of gold they sought."

Jim wrote, "gold?" in his notebook, then looked at
the word "INDIAN?" and underlined it. Jim had heard
years ago that Chrissie's father was a Cherokee, but
he had forgotten it until that moment. Chrissie had
gone to school in Aliceville until the third grade, when
she moved with her mother and father to the deep
mountains west of Asheville. From there they had
moved on to Oklahoma. Jim didn't remember much
about her, although she had been in his grade. Her
hair had been very long even then, and she had been
very quiet. His only vivid memory of her was of something that happened during recess just before she
moved away. It was the last day of school in the old
building, before the new building (the one in which
they now sat) opened the next fall. Jim had seen
Chrissie standing alone on the playground. Something
about the way she stood by herself had made him

angry, and a sudden fury had overcome him. Without knowing why, he had rushed up behind her and
shouted, "Have a nice TRIP!" before shoving her
down. Chrissie had skinned both knees and cried,
but she had not told on him. Jim was never punished,
although he felt he had deserved to be, and he never
told her he was sorry, although he had been. He
didn't see Chrissie again until the first day of school
this year, when he had watched her walk around the
front of the bus from Lynn's Mountain and up the
stairs toward him. And, without knowing why, he had
watched for her ever since.

The rest of the class passed slowly while Miss Brown
talked about her extended family and the occasional
Spanish explorer. The afternoon had grown hot and
still, the air rapidly thickening with the smell of teen-
agers ripening against their will in the heat, an odor
poorly masked by vanilla extract and cheap perfume
and scented hair oil. Several of the boys were sound
asleep, their heads down on their desks. Dennis Deane
picked something off the tip of his chin and tried
to show it to the girl sitting beside him, who refused
to look.

Jim leaned back and stretched. He tapped his pencil on his notebook. He glanced over at Norma Harris, his old girlfriend, with whom he had broken up
during the summer. She was getting a head start on
her math homework, which filled Jim with contempt.
Norma was pretty, probably the prettiest girl in Alice-

ville School, but she was a know-it-all. A goody-goody and a know-it-all and a cold fish. Her yellow hair was exactly the same color as Jim's, and for that reason, and because they both made good grades, people had always assumed that they would go together some day.

And so they had.

But Norma had barely let Jim kiss her, and never for very long, and he had gotten tired of arguing about it. She had absolutely refused to climb into the rumble seat of his car to look at the stars. The night he finally broke up with her, Norma had said, "I can see the stars from my house, Jim." That, somehow, had been the last straw. Some girls were just *too* religious. *I can see the stars from my house, Jim.* He didn't want an easy girlfriend, just one that was easier than Norma Harris. The girl actually had a picture of Abraham Lincoln on the wall in her bedroom. Jim had never set foot in Norma's bedroom, of course, but he had glimpsed Lincoln from the hallway. Mama was still upset with Jim for breaking up with Norma, but he didn't care. He had decided that he liked black hair better than blond anyway, especially when it was long.

Why *was* Chrissie's hair so long?

Jim considered the possible reasons. Maybe she was a member of the Holiness church. Holiness women weren't allowed to cut their hair. But most of the Holiness girls Jim knew piled their hair into elaborate, impossibly tall hairdos and kept it in place with complicated arrays of hairpins and bows, or even nets. Jim wrote, "HOLINESS?" in his notebook underneath

"INDIAN?" but then crossed it out, hoping it wasn't true. Holiness girls were even stricter than Baptist girls. A Holiness girl probably wouldn't let you kiss her at all until you married her. And then you'd still be kissing a Holiness girl, and she'd tell you not to mess up her hair and she'd want you to go to church for six hours every Sunday, and three hours on Wednesday night. You'd probably have to sit beside her father while she sat with the women on the opposite side of the church and waved her arms in the air and shouted in unknown tongues. Besides, Chrissie just didn't *seem* to be Holiness. He drew another, darker line through "HOLINESS?" and put another question mark after "INDIAN?" Jim knew that Mama would throw a fit if he ever tried to date a Holiness girl and wondered if she would throw a bigger one or a smaller one if he tried to date a Cherokee.

Chrissie shifted in her seat, and the hair lying on Jim's history book moved slightly and became a small, glossy animal curled and napping in the sun. A muskrat, Jim thought. No, a mink. No, a small, black fox. A kit. Jim wondered if a kit fox would bite you if you tried to pet it. He placed his left hand on his history book and drummed his fingers. He slowly slid his fingers up the page toward Chrissie's hair. Chrissie shifted again. The kit twitched in its sleep, dreaming of green fields lush with mice. Jim stopped. He felt his heart stuttering beneath his skin. He pursed his lips and almost inaudibly whispered, "Shh." The kit remained still. He moved his hand up the slick paper, a line, a half line at a time, through the Yankee blockade at Wilmington. Only the bravest blockade-running captains, under cover of darkness, were able to bring desperately needed supplies into the besieged port. Jim raised his middle finger and inched his hand forward until his finger was suspended above Chrissie's black hair. He took a deep breath. He lowered his finger and touched her hair as gently as he knew how to touch anything. He had never felt anything so soft.

Norma

WHEN THE bell rang, ending the day, Jim took his time heading home. He wandered slowly down the hallway while his schoolmates swirled noisily from the classrooms, their feet pounding on the wooden floors; he sauntered down the front steps while the fleeing students parted into streams around him. One by one his friends climbed onto the idling buses or walked down the hill toward town. Once the schoolyard was empty, the buses folded their doors and one at a time pulled away. The Lynn's Mountain bus was the last to leave. Chrissie Steppe sat by Ellie Something near the front and didn't look out the window toward Jim. The bus eased down the drive and turned right onto the state highway. Jim watched it disappear from sight; he listened until the drone of its engine and, finally, the last, happy shouts of its passengers simply vanished from earshot. Aliceville School suddenly seemed a lonely place. Somewhere inside, a teacher laughed, a ghostly sound in the nearly deserted building. A stray breeze blew one of the classroom doors closed, and the bang echoed through the hallway.

Jim reluctantly started for home and only then turned his attention to Norma Harris, who waited for him underneath the tall pine tree at the top of the driveway. Every Tuesday and Thursday she visited Jim's house to work on a quilt that she and his mother had started the previous winter. And Mama insisted that Jim be a gentleman and walk Norma down the hill. After he broke up with Norma, he had been shocked that his mother chose to continue working on the quilt, and shocked that Norma even wanted to finish it. When Jim complained about Norma's visits, his mother only shook her head and stared at him as if he needed a bath.

Jim could tell that Norma was angry with him as he crossed the schoolyard. She had been mad at him more or less continuously since he had broken up with her. This school year their walks down the hill to Jim's house had not been pleasant. He walked past Norma without acknowledging her; she fell in beside him without speaking. Her heels scuffed on the pavement as they descended the hill, making a sound that Jim had once found endearing but that now simply irritated him; once he had thought that the worn-down heels of Norma's shoes were cute, but now he thought they looked shabby.

"Everybody knows we're not dating anymore,"

Norma said. "You don't have to make me stand by myself like that. It's embarrassing."

"You know where I live," Jim said. "You don't have to wait on me if you don't want to."

Back when they were going together, Jim and Norma had walked down the hill holding hands almost every day. The teasing and needling spilling from the passing buses had simultaneously pleased and annoyed him. He had shouted at the boys hanging from the windows, but only halfheartedly; he had smiled proudly while his ears burned. In those days he occasionally let go of Norma's hand and tried to drop back a step just so he could watch her walk from behind. Watching her walk had made him want to grab her and kiss her over and over — although she wouldn't have let him if he had tried. Now he thought the way she walked made her look smug and bossy, the walk of a know-it-all, and he no longer wanted to kiss her. Jim could not understand how he could have loved Norma so much then and feel so differently now. His head seemed filled with memories belonging to another person, and he wished he could give them back.

"You act like it might kill you to be seen walking with me," Norma said.

"You act like you can't walk by yourself."

"When did you become so impolite?"

"Four score and seven years ago."

"Jerk," Norma said.

At the bottom of the hill, they had to pause at the

highway while three cars and a truck passed. The traffic seemed intentionally spaced to prolong their time together as much as possible.

When the last car went by, Jim bowed and extended his arm toward the highway. "After you," he said.

Norma lifted her chin and tossed her hair in response.

They crossed the road and cut through the fallow field that separated the highway from Depot Street, where Jim lived with his family. They walked on the path he had worn clean over the last eight years while walking to school. He saw his footprints from that morning, and some from the day before; he wondered, as he often had, why the path had never been quite straight. There was no reason it shouldn't be.

"I saw you today," Norma said.

"You saw me doing what?"

"I saw you playing with that Indian girl's hair."

Jim felt his cheeks go hot. "She's not an Indian," he said.

"She's half an Indian," Norma said.

"You don't know what she is."

"I know, among other things, that she's got hair like an Indian."

"So what? A lot of people have black hair. *Mama* has black hair."

"I know people call her daddy *Injun* Joe Steppe."

"Big deal," Jim said. "Uncle Zeno calls me Doc, but that doesn't mean I'm a doctor. Besides, so what if she is an Indian, or half an Indian, or whatever you said."

"Maybe she's not somebody you should get tangled up with, that's what."

"And you are, I suppose."

"Well," she said, "I *was*."

"Why are we even having this discussion? Chrissie Steppe is not my girlfriend. She's Bucky Bucklaw's girlfriend. Everybody knows that. I've never said ten words to her in my whole life. I don't even know her daggum middle name, or anything else about her. So, why don't you just mind your own business?"

Norma stopped in her tracks. "Look at me," she said.

Jim looked instead at his shoes. They were dusty from the path through the field.

"Jim Glass, you look at me right this minute."

He looked up and watched Norma study his face as if she were about to spit on her finger and rub off a streak of dirt.

"Good Lord," she said.

"What?"

"You're in love with her."

"I am not."

"You are, too."

"I am not. I don't even know her. How could I be in love with her?"

"Then why is your face red?"

"I don't *know*, Norma. Because you're staring at me.

Because you're bothering me. Leave a boy alone, for gosh sakes, why don't you?"

Norma's eyes briefly clouded over. "I can't believe this," she said. "You break up with me and now you're in love with that . . ."

Jim almost smiled. He knew that Norma wanted to use a curse word, and also that she wouldn't.

". . . that *Cherokee*."

Jim shook his head in disgust and turned toward home.

Norma grabbed his arm. "Jim," she said. "Listen to me. I know you won't believe this, but I'm telling you this for your own good. You should stay away from Chrissie Steppe."

"Why?"

"Because I've *heard* things."

"What things?"

"Things I can't tell you."

"You don't know any more about her than I do."

"I know that a nice girl wouldn't let her hair fall all over some boy's desk, and then sit there while he plays with it. Especially when she's got a boyfriend in the navy."

"It's just hair," Jim said. "It landed on my desk by accident and she didn't know it. I was moving it so I could read about Wilmington."

The shadow of a smile passed across Norma's face. "That's the most ridiculous thing I ever heard," she said.

"Just leave me alone, Norma."

Uncle Zeno's house had never seemed farther away. Jim stopped when he reached the front steps. Norma brushed past him and climbed onto the porch.

"Tell Mama I'm going out to the mill to see Uncle Zeno," Jim said.

Norma opened the screen door, paused for a moment, and turned around. "Marie," she said.

"What?"

"Marie. That's Chrissie Steppe's middle name."

What Strange Country

*J*IM BACKED his Ford out of the shed behind Uncle Coran's store and eased it around the side of the building. He knew that Mama was more than likely listening at the screen door to the manner in which he drove away. Early on he had made the mistake of bragging about the power of the car's V8 engine, and since then, Mama regularly threatened to take away his key. She religiously complained to anyone who would listen, especially the uncles, that a Ford V8 was just too much car for a teenage boy to handle. After all, she said, John Dillinger had driven Ford V8s, and look what happened to *him*. Jim was sure Mama talked about the gangster just to make him nuts. Dillinger had been shot down coming out of a movie; he hadn't been anywhere *near* a Ford V8. And besides, whatever it had been that made John Dillinger go bad, it had certainly not been his *car*. Still, Jim drove with the decorum of an undertaker within earshot of Mama.

The dirt lot in front of the store was empty, and the

CLOSED sign hung from its wire on the doorknob.
Uncle Coran occasionally closed early on slow afternoons, and Jim was glad he didn't have to talk to
anyone just yet. He stopped at the edge of the state
highway and made a show of looking both ways. He
pulled delicately onto the road and shifted peacefully
up through the gears until he reached the ridiculous
Mama-mandated speed limit of thirty-five miles per
hour. The car, a 1935 coupe the uncles had given Jim
on his sixteenth birthday, was a dull, lusterless green,
but Jim liked the color because he thought it gave the
Ford something of a military look. He had dubbed
the car "The Major," a nickname Uncle Al had eventually painted in white cursive letters just beneath the
driver's-side window.

The intersection of the railroad tracks and the state
highway marked for Jim the point beyond which he
figured he was safe from Mama's nosiness. He kept the
speedometer steadily on thirty-five as he approached
the crossing sign and hit the railroad bed without
slowing down. Jim bounced out of his seat toward the
ceiling and savored the brief airborne sensation he
felt in his stomach. Once across the tracks, he downshifted into second gear and pushed the accelerator
all the way to the floor. When he popped the clutch,
the resulting roar from the Major made him smile
for the first time since fifth period. Soon Jim was traveling at sixty miles per hour, a mile a minute, pretty
much the Major's top speed on level ground. He
leaned forward to let the wind whistling through the

windows cool the sweat pasting his shirt to his back. On both sides of the road, cotton rows clicked past kaleidoscopically, each revealing for a fraction of a moment the full secret of its carefully hoed length. The Major's tires hummed on the smooth concrete.

Although Jim liked driving the Major fast more than just about anything, he soon felt his anger at Norma gaining ground on his attempt to flee it. *"Jim,"* he said, mimicking Norma's voice, *"I know you won't believe this, but I'm telling you this for your own good. You should stay away from Chrissie Steppe."* He pushed the accelerator harder against the floorboard, but the Major refused to go any faster. He slapped the steering wheel in frustration.

"Daggummit, Norma!" he shouted. "Leave me alone!

"I can't believe this," he whimpered. *"You're in love with that, that Cherokee.*

"So what if I am?" he answered. "It's none of your damn business who I'm in love with."

Jim paused in his argument with the imaginary Norma. The Major slowed involuntarily. *I'm in love with Chrissie Steppe,* he thought, allowing himself to fully consider the possibility for the first time. He realized that the idea had been a shadow inside his head for so long that it had become familiar. Now, by attaching itself to words, it had taken on solid form and stepped into the light. "Hello," it seemed to be saying, "you know who I am."

Something warm inflated and rose inside his chest,

replacing in a single moment his ill temper with a growing elation. "I love Chrissie Steppe," he said out loud, realizing as he did so that the words were carrying him over some momentous boundary he had never known existed. Jim didn't know in what strange country this unexpected crossing landed him, or what dangers faced him, only that he found the vistas glorious to consider. He didn't know how it was possible that he loved Chrissie Steppe, only that he did. He didn't wonder whether Chrissie would, or even could, ever love him back. Nor did he think for more than a fleeting second about Bucky Bucklaw, floating on his lunkhead boat somewhere in the Pacific Ocean. For now, all that lay far below him. He leaned over so that he could see out the passenger window all the way to the top of Lynn's Mountain, which rose to the north and west of the highway. Chrissie lived up there somewhere, and for a moment he imagined her waiting for him, watching his tiny car inch along the road in the valley far below. He blew the horn as if she could hear it. Then he blew it again. He wanted to yell something to her, but couldn't bring himself to direct the words *I love you* toward the mountain. Not yet, anyway. Instead he yelled, *"Conquistador!"* which was the first word that came into his mind.

When Jim reached the Lynn's Mountain turnoff, he jerked the wheel sharply to the right and felt the Major's tires leave the pavement and scramble uncertainly onto the dirt road. He again downshifted into second and popped the clutch, but this time he winced, when the Major's engine bellowed in complaint. He had been going too fast to downshift and could have blown the motor. He let off the gas, cocked an ear toward the engine, and listened carefully. Once satisfied that the motor had not come unraveled, he stomped again on the accelerator and whipped the wheel to the left and to the right, joyously sliding through a short series of fishtails. Like most boys who did the majority of their driving on dirt roads, Jim liked to think that he could drive as well sideways as he could in a straight line. He slowed only when he approached the turnoff to Uncle Zeno's mill. Uncle Zeno understood that Jim, like most boys, was occasionally going to drive too fast, but he had also made it clear that he never wanted to catch Jim doing it. Jim looked wistfully in the rearview mirror at the thick cloud of red dust drifting in the Major's wake. He responsibly stuck his arm out the window, signaled a left turn, and pulled sedately off the road and into the yard of the mill, where, surprisingly, all three of the uncles' trucks were parked.

The mill was a wide, whitewashed building made of rough lumber, roofed with moss-covered oak shingles the uncles had split themselves years before. Across the front of the mill, MCBRIDE was painted in large, fading black letters. When Jim walked inside, he found the uncles sitting on straight chairs at the edge of the loft with their .22 rifles on their laps. A thin cloud of gun smoke nosed through the dust particles rising steadily toward the sunlit windows; the sharp smell of the burned powder blended oddly with the warm, sweet smell of ground corn.

"Halt!" Uncle Coran called out. "Who goes there?"

"John Dillinger," Jim said.

"Well," Uncle Coran said. "You know what happened to him."

"He got in trouble for driving his car like a knot-head," said Uncle Zeno.

"You heard me coming?" Jim asked.

"People in Virginia heard you coming," said Uncle Al. "Did you blow the motor?"

"The Major's fine," Jim said. "It's going to take more than a little downshift to kill the Major."

"We ain't going to put a new motor in that car," Uncle Zeno said. "You remember that. Your mama would have all our hides."

"You won't have to."

"So make yourself useful," Uncle Coran said. "Go get your gun."

Uncle Zeno's gristmill, despite the best efforts of a sizable contingent of half-wild cats, was beset with rats. Jim had learned to hunt by shooting rats from the mill loft, and he had no idea how many he had killed over the years. He returned to the Major and pulled his .22 from behind the seat. He removed the magazine tube from the rifle, emptied the shells into his free hand, and put them in his pocket. Back in-side the mill, he took another chair from around the stove, handed it up to Uncle Zeno, then climbed the steep, open stairs to the loft, carrying his rifle. Jim sat down beside Uncle Zeno, who passed him five rat-shot cartridges. Jim loaded the cartridges into the magazine, levered a round into the chamber, and set the hammer on half cock. He squinted down into the dimly lit machinery of the grinding room.

"Who's winning?" he asked.

"I think Zeno is," said Uncle Coran. "By my count, he's got four. Al's got two and I've got two."

Uncle Al snorted.

Uncle Coran pointed at a dead rat lying along the far wall. "That one's under protest," he said. "Al says they shot him at the same time."

"Tie goes to the runner," Uncle Al said.

"But I'm pretty sure Zeno shot him first," said Uncle Coran.

Uncle Zeno winked at Jim. "One more, Doc, and I'll be an ace."

"The score's three and a half to two and a half to two, and you know it," Uncle Al said. "One more and *I'm* tied for first."

Uncle Coran turned and stared at Uncle Al. "Allie, do you honestly think it's possible to kill *half* a rat?"

"You never could count," mumbled Uncle Al.

Uncle Zeno winked again at Jim. "Is Norma at the house?" he asked.

"Afraid so."

"Figured that's why you were here."

Jim leaned forward as his eyes became accustomed to the shadowy room. The sun drew soft yellow pictures of the streaked windows on the floor. Gradually, he was able to locate the rest of the rat corpses scattered around. The immobile humps had obviously once been alive and were now just as obviously dead. He quickly scanned the holes in the floor and along the baseboards where he knew the rats came into the mill but saw nothing moving. Outside he could hear the lazy groan of metal and the rhythmic *splash-splash-splash* of water falling as the great iron wheel turned.

"Norma and Mama are about to drive me crazy," he said.

"You stepped in that pile all by yourself," Uncle Zeno said.

"Daggummit," Jim said. "I didn't step in anything. I don't have to date Norma Harris if I don't want to date Norma Harris."

"Shh," said Uncle Al.

"Don't raise your voice," said Uncle Zeno. "And I'm not saying you do. I'm just saying a lot of people got their feelings hurt when you broke up with Norma, your mama included."

"Well, I don't see what the big deal is."

"The big deal is," Uncle Zeno went on, "that Norma *chose* you. You understand what I'm saying? She picked you *out*. She decided you were the only boy in the world for her, although I don't quite understand that."

"There's no accounting for taste," said Uncle Coran.

"But we were just *dating*."

"*You* were just dating, Jim. Norma was picking. And when she picked you, your mama picked her. Norma was going to be the daughter she never had. That's what that quilt was about."

"It's just a quilt," said Jim.

"That's where you're wrong, Doc," Uncle Zeno said. "You're wrong as you can be about that. I told Coran and Al when your mama and Norma started in on that thing, I said, 'Boys, that quilt's gonna bring a world of trouble. You mark my word.'"

"I still don't see what the big deal is," Jim said.

Uncle Zeno swallowed. "Norma was making that quilt for your bed, Jim, and your mama was helping her."

Jim frowned. "I already got a quilt," he said. "I got three or four quilts."

Uncle Al shook his head. "He ain't too bright, is he?" he said.

"Hush, Allie," Uncle Coran said. "Here comes the good part."

"Jim, you're not listening to me. For your *bed*, you big knothead. For after you and Norma got married."

"*Married?*" Jim said. "Who said anything about *married?*"

"Daggummit, hold it down," said Uncle Al. "You're gonna scare every rat in this country off."

"Who said anything about married?"

"Did you tell Norma you loved her?" Uncle Zeno asked.

Jim blushed and looked away.

"Did you?"

Uncle Al shifted uncomfortably. "I don't need to hear this," he said.

"I guess so," said Jim.

"Well, Doc, that's all she needed to hear," Uncle Zeno said. "Norma's a serious girl. Some girls run around with boys for fun, but Norma's not one of those girls. You tell a girl like Norma you love her, you better be ready to marry her because she's gonna piece you a quilt."

"I didn't ask nobody to make me no daggum quilt."

Uncle Coran suddenly raised his rifle. The contested rat was trying to drag itself along the far wall. When Uncle Coran pulled the trigger, Jim saw the orange muzzle blast lick out into the dim light. The percussive, splitting report was surprisingly loud inside the enclosed room. It always was.

"Ha!" Uncle Coran shouted. "That rat wasn't dead. *I* killed it. That makes the score three to three to two. Now I'm tied for the lead."

"Ain't no doggone way," Uncle Al said. "Ain't no doggone way you're counting that."

Uncle Coran stared at Uncle Al in disbelief. "Now you're going to tell me you killed a *third* of a rat?"

"Yes, that's exactly what I'm telling you."

"Well, a minute ago you said it was half a rat. Seems to me you're losing rat by the minute."

"Cheater," Uncle Al said.

"Cheater?" said Uncle Coran. "How do you figure I'm a cheater? That rat was alive and I killed it."

"Boys," said Uncle Zeno.

Uncle Al levered three shells out of his rifle onto the loft floor. "If that's how it's going to be, I quit," he said. "I ain't going to play in no rigged game." He laid his rifle in his lap and crossed his arms. The uncles sat and stared silently into space. After a while Uncle Al leaned over, picked up the shells, and loaded them back into his rifle.

Jim wanted to smile but knew better. "Why are y'all killing rats, anyway?" he asked.

Uncle Zeno turned toward him. "Did you see that troop train this morning?"

"Yeah. Me and Dennis Deane and them were standing on the steps."

Uncle Al shook his head. "Here we go again. Daggummit."

"I don't see why y'all are killing rats over a troop train," Jim said. "We're not fighting anybody."

"No, but we're getting ready to," said Uncle Zeno. "You just wait. If Hitler invades England, we'll be knee-deep in that mess."

"And don't forget the Japs are getting bowed up, too," added Uncle Al.

"I think we ought to invade South Carolina," Uncle Coran said. "I never did like it down there. The people are peculiar."

"But Roosevelt said he was going to keep us out of the war," said Jim.

"Yeah, I know what he said, but cotton prices have started up," Uncle Zeno said.

"Cotton prices? I don't understand. Isn't cotton going up a good thing?"

"Not necessarily, Doc. You've got to wonder why now, all of a sudden."

Jim thought. "Uniforms?"

"Uniforms. Tents. Somebody somewhere has already decided to do something they ain't told us about yet."

"Puttees," said Uncle Coran. "Don't forget about puttees."

"Puttees," said Uncle Al. "I *hate* puttees. Daggummit."

As it grew too dark to shoot, Jim left the uncles sitting glumly in the loft — before they could ask him to pick up the rats — and headed back to town. It was almost suppertime. On this trip he drove so slowly that he could hear the songs of solitary crickets rising along the shoulder of the highway as he approached, and falling away as he passed. The road and the surrounding fields lay in cool shadow but the top half of Lynn's Mountain still warmed itself in the sun. Jim pulled off the road for a minute and watched the evening advance toward the ridgetop. The air was so clear, the light so fine, that the shapes of the individual trees blanketing the upper slopes separated themselves from their brothers and stepped forward for Jim to count or admire. He picked out a tree and watched until the shadow line climbed past it. The great love for Chrissie Steppe he had discovered on the drive out had already been tempered by the uncles' war talk, and by the knowledge that he might be forced to leave her behind, maybe before he could tell her how he felt. He didn't know for sure where she lived — he thought it was somewhere near the Bucklaws — and even if he turned around and drove as fast as he could, it would be dark long before he got there.

When Jim reached town he parked the Major underneath the shed and walked slowly down Depot Street, beneath the blank windows of the school, toward home. Tomorrow morning he would stand on the landing with his friends, and Chrissie would step off the bus from the mountain. It wasn't much, but it was something. It was a start. He wiped his feet carefully on the back porch, dropped his books on the bench by the door, and stepped into the kitchen. After the cool of the evening, the room seemed almost unbearably hot from Mama's cooking. A big pot of pintos simmered on top of the stove; he opened the warming cabinet and found two pones of corn bread and a peach cobbler. Jim swallowed hungrily. He was very fond of pinto beans and corn bread, particularly with chopped onion and a big glass of buttermilk.

He found Mama in her bedroom. She had laid the quilt that she and Norma were making on top of her bed and was studying it critically.

"Decided it was finally safe to come home, did you?" she asked.

"That's about right," said Jim.

"We finished piecing the top today. What do you think?"

"I like it," he said, which was the truth.

The pattern of the quilt was called "Schoolhouse," although Jim thought the buildings Mama and Norma had pieced together looked more like houses or cabins than they did schoolhouses. They were cut so that they seemed viewed from an angle; one long side and one gable end of each were visible; each house had two doors on the long side and a yellow window in the gable; each roof had two red chimneys. The walls and roofs of each house were cut from different fabrics, mostly from printed flour sacks that Mama and Norma had collected or traded other flour sacks for, although here and there Jim recognized a piece of cloth from a dress that Mama used to wear, or one of his old shirts. The few pieces he didn't recognize had come from Norma's family. The houses were set onto squares of dark blue; the squares, separated by rich, red sashing, were arranged in five rows of four squares each.

Mama reached into her apron pocket and pulled out her pair of good scissors. When she sewed she wore small gold glasses on the end of her nose that made her look older than she was. She leaned over the quilt and snipped off a stray piece of thread that Jim never would have noticed.

"It looks like a town," Jim said, tracing a path along the background in between the squares. "The red looks like streets."

"I think so, too," said Mama. "That's what I like about it."

"Why are all the windows yellow?"

"That shows that somebody's home. They look too lonesome without a light on inside."

"Where do you live?" Jim asked.

Mama studied Jim for a moment before pointing to the third house in the second row. It had light blue walls of faded chambray. "Right there," she said, flushing slightly. "Do you know where that cloth came from?"

Jim knew but didn't say anything.

"From one of your father's shirts," she said.

She ran a finger over the fabric before suddenly smacking Jim three times on the arm, not quite playfully.

"Oh, daggum your fickle hide, Jim Glass. That's the last piece of that shirt I had."

"Ow," Jim said. "Nobody told you to put that cloth in Norma's quilt, now, did they?"

"I just feel like beating you half to death right now."

"Did they? Tell the truth."

Mama put her hands on her hips. "No," she said. "Nobody told me to use the last piece of your dead father's shirt in this quilt. Let's just say that because of the actions and words of a certain young man last winter regarding a certain young lady, I felt safe in making certain assumptions."

"Well, you know what they say about assuming, don't you?"

"Humph," Mama said. "There's only one A-S-S in this room right now, young man, and it's not me."

Jim laughed. "Where do I live?"

"I'm not sure you're still welcome in this town."

"Well, where was I going to live, before you ran me off?"

Mama pointed at a house in the third row, across the street from her own.

"Was Norma going to live there, too?"

Mama shook her head briskly and snipped at Jim with her scissors.

"You're trying my patience, mister," she said. "I'm warning you."

"You could always stop working on the quilt."

Mama rolled her eyes at the ceiling. "You don't have any idea why I'm doing this, do you?"

"No, ma'am," Jim said. "I don't have any idea."

"What I'm trying to do is let that poor girl escape this whole fiasco with a little dignity intact. But you probably can't understand that."

"I guess I can understand that," Jim said.

For a moment he felt a little bad about making Norma wait underneath the tree until all the school buses had passed. He resolved to do better. Maybe on Tuesdays and Thursdays he could hurry and get Norma down the hill before the buses finished loading.

The uncles clomped onto the back porch and stomped their feet on the mat.

"What were they all doing out at the mill?" Mama asked.

"Shooting rats," Jim said.

Mama frowned. "How come?"

"I think they were upset about that troop train this morning. They think we're about to get in the war."

"The president's going to keep us out of the war."

"What if he doesn't?" Jim asked.

"That's easy," Mama said. "I won't let you go."

BOOK II

The Secrets of Women

Call to Glory

*T*HE WEATHER was still warm — the days mild, the first frost still days or weeks away — but the world seemed bent on practicing for the coming winter. This morning the clouds resembled snow clouds, but instead of snow they produced a steady gray mist that absorbed sound and discouraged ambition. People all over Aliceville rose, stared out at the day, and lit fires they did not need.

Among the loafers smoking in the store, Uncle Coran tried to incite a disagreement about whether the precipitation falling outside was a heavy fog or a light drizzle, but he found no takers. Mama grew sleepy after the midday meal and left the dishes soaking in the sink. Uncle Zeno drove slowly toward New Carpenter with the idea of buying a new logging chain but, because he didn't really need a new logging chain, thought better of it, circled the courthouse, and drove slowly home. Uncle Al found himself sitting on a crate, staring out the wide door of the mule barn. He had no idea how long he had been there. He stood up and dusted off the legs of his overalls, even though he had put them on clean that morning and had done no real work to speak of.

Jim spent the day staring distractedly into the gloom. He paid little attention to anything that was said in his classes. When the bell rang ending each period, he moved on to the next classroom, took his seat, and stared again out the window. Each new window changed the perspective from which he viewed the world but did nothing to improve it. The mist had reduced the woods on the far side of the bottoms into mere suggestion. The trees were discernible only sporadically, like the memory of something pleasant that happened a long time ago.

The weather matched Jim's mood perfectly. He found it a good day to labor under the almost public burden of a not-quite-secret unrequited love. His friends, both the guys on the steps and the girls who pretended to be offended by their existence, had begun to tease him about Christine Steppe — which genuinely puzzled Jim because he had spoken of his feelings about Chrissie to no one, and certainly not to Dennis Deane, who these days, when the bus from Lynn's Mountain pulled up in front of the school, launched into a ridiculous, mincing recitation of "Jim and Chrissie sitting in a tree" that even Jim had to admit was funny. The only person with anything resembling direct knowledge about Jim's great "secret" was Norma Harris, and Jim knew that Norma was unlikely to have tattled. Complaining about Chrissie would have made Norma look bad, and besides, Norma was nothing if not discreet. (Had she been the kind of girl who worried less about public appearance and was occasionally indiscreet, Jim might not have broken up with her in the first place.) He didn't bother denying the accusations about Chrissie when they arose, because in each instance he secretly hoped that his lack of a denial would twist itself into a declaration by the time she heard about it.

And he counted on her hearing about it.

Because Chrissie had a boyfriend (even an absent one he neither liked nor respected), Jim believed he had to wait for Chrissie to confront him about the rumors before he could honorably tell her how he felt. He had no respect for guys who snaked away other guys' girlfriends, or attempted to, although he now longed for a loophole — such as Chrissie calling him out — that would allow him to become a snake without appearing to be. For her part, however, Chrissie showed little inclination to talk to him at all, let alone raise the question of whether or not he loved her.

When Chrissie didn't show up for Miss Brown's class, Jim sat up alertly for the first time all day. He scooted his desk away from hers, put his feet on the back rung of her chair, and stared at the door until he was sure she wasn't coming through it. He had seen Chrissie periodically throughout the day — in addition to history they had two other classes together, although their desks weren't close by in those classes — but now she had stepped out of the familiar track in which they all marched through the days. Jim knew that, not being outgoing and popular (like Norma), she wasn't the kind of girl who one of the teachers would have held out of class to paint posters or carry notes here or there, and he couldn't think of anywhere else she could be. He looked around the room when Miss Brown called Chrissie's name from the roll, but no one else seemed to be wondering where Chrissie had gotten to, nor care about the fact that he was wondering.

When Miss Brown told the class to open their books, Norma glanced up at him, tilted her head to one side, and sighed in commiseration at . . . what? The long day, the bleak weather, the heavy volume of English homework? Jim didn't know. But when she blushed and looked down quickly at her book, he knew that he had somehow responded to her friendly look with what had appeared to be a hostile one of his own. That had not been his intent. He had only been concerned about Chrissie, and facing an hour of Miss Brown's rambling without Chrissie at the desk in front of his, without her hair falling onto his history book, he would have welcomed any friendly gesture, even one that he might have regretted responding to later. He stared at Norma for a while, hoping to make up, but she did not look at him again. The weather naturally caused Miss Brown to forget about taxation without representation and drone on instead about the moors of England, which to Jim sounded more like a disagreeable family than a disagreeable place. In his notebook he wrote, "BEWARE THE MOORES OF ENGLAND!"

When the bell rang ending the day, he stood on the landing at the top of the steps and watched for Chrissie. But she did not appear among the stream of students who drained out the school and filled up the buses. When the Lynn's Mountain bus shut its doors and pulled forward through the mist, Jim felt a worry roll itself into a ball inside his chest. He knew that Chrissie had no other way up the mountain. As the bus passed his place on the steps and started down the drive, Ellie Something leaned out a window and yelled, *"She's sick. She needs a ride home."* Jim nodded and waved in response. Because of the nature of Ellie Something's news, he was only mildly irritated that even the freshmen of Aliceville School now seemed to know his business. He turned, and, without thinking, pulled open the door and strode into the building.

When Jim walked into the office, Mr. Dunlap, the principal, and Mrs. Murray, the secretary, were laughing about something, but they stopped when they saw him.

"Yes, Mr. Glass?" Mr. Dunlap said.

"I heard that Christine Steppe was sick."

"Yes?"

"And that she needed a ride home."

"You heard correctly, I suppose," said the principal. "Are you volunteering for the job?"

"Yes, sir," Jim said. "I have a car."

Mr. Dunlap and Mrs. Murray looked at each other. Mr. Dunlap winked and Mrs. Murray not very successfully stifled a smile. Jim felt his ears go red.

"Okay, Jim," Mr. Dunlap said. "Provided Miss Steppe is agreeable. I frankly didn't know how we were going to get her up the mountain." He pointed across the hall at the nurse's office. "She's resting in there."

Because Aliceville School didn't have a nurse on staff, the nurse's office was used infrequently — most often when the severe-looking woman from the county office showed up to check the heads of the poor kids for lice. The room held an ancient hospital bed, a beat-up steel cabinet, and a single, punitive-looking chair; in the corner lurked the rusting metal wastebasket that Mrs. Murray or one of the teachers unceremoniously thrust at sick children during moments of crisis. The only picture on the walls was a print called *Call to Glory*, torn from a magazine during the Great War, in which a nurse held the hand of a comatose doughboy while above them the soldier's spirit marched triumphantly up a sunbeam toward George Washington and Abraham Lincoln, who waited to greet him knee-deep in a radiant cloud. The nurse's office was — according to the story older students told to frighten first-graders — haunted by the ghost of a little boy who stuck a marble up his nose and accidentally sucked it down his windpipe.

Jim found the door slightly ajar. He tapped on it twice and slowly pushed it open. Chrissie lay curled up on the bed, facing the wall, her knees clutched to her stomach. He heard her moan softly.

"Christine?" he said. He was surprised at how soft his voice sounded.

Chrissie raised her head and looked at him over her shoulder. Jim saw her pupils widen.

"Oh, no," she said. "Get out of here."

"Chrissie?"

"Right now."

"I've come to give you a ride home."

She moaned again. "You've what?"

"Come to give you a ride home."

"Have you gone completely insane?"

"No," Jim said. "I've got a car."

She didn't respond.

Jim eased farther into the room. "The bus just left," he said. "How else are you going to get up the mountain?"

She didn't respond.

He drew the uncomfortable-looking chair away from the wall and placed it beside the bed. Sad gray light settled on the bed from the single window high up on the wall. Chrissie's hair lay spread in disarray on the white sheet. Jim hoped it wouldn't get tangled.

"Don't sit down," Chrissie said.

"Okay. I won't."

"Put the chair back."

"Okay," he said. "It's back."

"Is your car here?"

"No. It's down at the store."

"Go get it," Chrissie said.

Jim first jogged to the store and from the doorway told Uncle Coran that Mr. Dunlap had asked him to give a ride home to a sick kid. (As he told the story, Jim hoped it was close enough to the truth to keep him out of trouble. The loafers at the store — as Jim had hoped — kept Uncle Coran from quizzing him too closely; Mama would have demanded a fuller explanation and perhaps forbidden him to go.) When he stopped the Major in front of the school, one of the red doors swung open and Chrissie stepped out. Her skin looked unnaturally pale, and Jim thought that, were the nurse's office really haunted, *that's* what the ghost would look like. She walked down the stairs with the exaggerated care of someone navigating an icy sidewalk. Jim leaned over and pushed open the passenger-side door. Chrissie placed her books on the seat between them. Once she closed the door, she wrapped her arms around her abdomen, closed her eyes, and leaned against the window.

"Don't talk to me," she said. "I'm about to throw up."

"Okay, then," Jim said.

Not talking, however, was the last thing Jim wanted to do. Speaking privately to Chrissie at school was out of the question, of course, and running into her around town was unlikely because she lived on Lynn's Mountain. By Jim's reckoning, this might be his only opportunity to talk to her alone, ever. He could feel thousands of words, everything that he wanted to say to her, piled up behind his teeth, waiting for him to open his mouth so they could storm into the light.

Instead he said, "Here we go."

At the highway, he waited to let a single car pass, although he could have beaten it easily. Sitting at the stop sign in the Major greatly increased his chances of being spotted — and perhaps waved down — by Mama, but Jim wanted the trip to last as long as possible. He nervously watched the front door of Uncle Zeno's house and drummed his fingers on the wheel. The approaching car, an ancient Marathon, eventually clattered by. Jim pulled onto the highway behind it and shifted languidly up through the gears to a speed even Mama would have approved of.

At the railroad crossing he slowed the Major to a near crawl and bumped gingerly across the tracks. Chrissie still leaned against the window and he didn't want her to bang her head against the glass. But once he reached the turnoff to the Lynn's Mountain road, he couldn't resist downshifting and throwing the Major into a single lazy fishtail. (He suspected that Norma had secretly liked fishtailing, although she had always demanded that he stop.) Chrissie whirled on him angrily.

"What's the matter with you?" she asked. "Do you think that's funny? Are you trying to make me throw up?"

Jim slowed the car so quickly that it almost stalled and he had to downshift into first.

"No," he said. "No. I'm sorry. I wasn't thinking."

While Jim looked at Chrissie, her skin changed in an instant from a not-so-healthy-looking pale into a desperately unhealthy-looking gray. Sweat bloomed on her cheek and above her upper lip.

"Oh, no," she said, leaning forward and placing her head on the Major's dashboard.

"What?"

"Ohh," she moaned.

"Are you going to be sick?"

Chrissie sat up straight, looked around wildly, then lay back against the seat and tightly shut her eyes. "No," she said. "I'm fine. Keep driving."

She moaned again.

"Hold on," Jim said. He steered the car across the bridge over Painter Creek.

"Stop the car," she said.

"Right now?"

"Stop the car."

Jim jerked the wheel to the right, and before the Major even stopped rolling, Chrissie leapt out and disappeared into the thick rhododendron that lined the stream's steep banks. Jim didn't see how any creature could have vanished into a tangle of rhododendron so easily, especially a full-grown girl wearing a skirt. When he turned off the engine, he heard her crashing through the thicket toward the creek bed. He imagined that must be what a deer sounded like. Jim knew what rabbits and squirrels sounded like, but all the deer in his part of the world had been shot years before.

He sat behind the wheel until he heard Chrissie stop running, then he opened the door and climbed onto the running board. He cocked an ear toward the rhododendron and listened. The woods were quiet; at first he couldn't hear anything, save the indifferent murmur of the creek. Then, somewhere near the water, he heard Chrissie gag. He felt a tearing sensation, a great helplessness, rip through his chest. He ran around the car and squinted into the rhododendron, but he couldn't see her. More than anything, he wanted to help, but he had no idea what to do.

"Chrissie," he called. "Chrissie! Are you all right?"

She gagged again. When she finally answered him she sounded desperate. "Don't you dare come down here!" she said. "You stay right where you are!"

"Where are you?" Jim asked.

"I mean it!" Chrissie yelled. "I said no!" She started to say something else, but coughed and was ill again.

Jim moved to the edge of the roadside and looked for a way into the rhododendron. "I'm coming in," he said.

"No!" Chrissie screamed.

Jim fidgeted toward the thicket, but didn't move forward. "Okay," he called. "Ready or not, here I come!" (And would wonder for the rest of his life why he had said *that*.)

A rock sailed up out of the rhododendron and plunked into the road. "Damn you! I'll kill you if you take another step!"

Jim clapped his hands against the side of his head. He turned around in a circle. "But you're *sick*," he said. "You shouldn't have to be sick by yourself. Nobody should. Let me come down there."

Another rock flew up out of the trees. This one landed with a clank on the roof of the Major and bounced onto the road.

"Hey!" Jim yelled. "Take it easy on the car!"

"I'll kill you deader than hell, Jim Glass! So help me God. I'm warning you for the last time!"

Jim heard Chrissie scrambling around for another rock. He heard a hysterical-sounding giggle bubble up out of his mouth and wondered why Chrissie Steppe throwing rocks at his car made him feel like laughing.

"All right," he said. "Don't shoot. I give up."

While Chrissie climbed up out of the rhododendron, Jim surreptitiously examined the round dent on the roof of the Major and, to his surprise, found that it didn't bother him very much. In fact, he didn't care about it at all. When she appeared at the edge of the thicket, he took her hand and helped her into the roadway. Her hand felt cold and clammy, not at all the way Jim had imagined it would feel, but he was glad to be holding it, anyway. Chrissie still looked desperately pale, but much better than she had when she had run into the rhododendron. He opened the door for her. Before he closed it he removed his handkerchief from his back pocket and offered it to her. He had been carrying one only since he became a senior, but until that moment he'd found no use for it.

"You can wipe your mouth off with this," he said. "I haven't used it. I mean, it's clean."

Chrissie accepted the handkerchief and stared at it. "Thank you," she said.

Between the bridge and the valley at the foot of the mountain, the road halfheartedly trailed the creek through a range of short, rolling hills. Sometimes it dipped down through the laurel and rhododendron and ran just above the level of the water, but other times it climbed away, so that not even the ravine that carried the creek was visible. When it curved through the woods, the straight black trunks of the trees loomed somberly in the mist. A few yellow poplar leaves lay pasted to the roadway and softly hissed beneath the Major's tires; their sweet, melancholy smell affirmed the coming of the hard frosts and cold winds that would strip the trees bare. Jim opened his window a crack. He was afraid that the curves and the rise and fall of the road would make Chrissie sick again, so he drove very slowly.

"It's okay," Chrissie said. "It's over now. You can speed up."

Jim glanced over at her. Her color had almost fully

returned, and in general she seemed to be a different person, perhaps someone it might be safe to talk to.

"What do you think was the matter?" he asked.

Chrissie shook her head. "I'm fine now."

"Do you think it's the flu?" Both of Jim's maternal grandparents had died of the flu in 1918, and Mama had reared Jim to expect the worst regarding sudden illnesses.

"No, it's not the flu," she said.

"Maybe you just ate something that didn't agree with you."

Chrissie slapped her palms twice against her legs. *"Jim . . . ,"* she said.

"What?"

"Listen to me. It's not the flu and I didn't eat anything that disagreed with me. Okay? *Now* do you understand?"

"I don't think so," he said.

Chrissie covered her eyes with her fists. She sighed deeply. "I'm only going to say this one time, all right?"

Jim nodded.

"It's my *P-E-R-I-O-D.*"

Jim mouthed the letters. When the letters bunched themselves into a word, he swallowed hard and stared straight ahead at the road. "Ah," he said. "Okay. All right. I see."

Chrissie looked away and stared out the window. They were passing a poor upland farm stacked precariously on the side of a red, barren-looking ridge.

The pasture was so steep it looked painted onto the hillside.

"Well," she said. "I don't see how they ever got grass to grow on the side of a bank like that."

They stared at the farm like pilgrims on reaching a site they had traveled thousands of miles to see.

"They used to have a white cow," Jim said.

"A what?"

"A white cow."

Chrissie started to laugh.

"Well," said Jim. "They did."

They settled into an embarrassing but not unwelcome silence. Jim was at least glad the subject had changed. He tried to think of something else to talk about, but before he came up with anything, he felt Chrissie looking at him. When he sneaked a look at her, her brow was dipped into a furious V.

"Promise me you won't ever tell a soul we talked about my you-know-what," she said.

"Trust me," Jim said. "You don't ever have to worry about that."

The Abandoned House

THE NEXT farmstead they passed lay deserted. Stickweed and broom sedge and ragweed and small, scraggly pine trees loitered about the yard and pasture; the roof of the barn had fallen in, and a nest of poison oak vines, their leaves turning a bloody red, seemed intent on pulling the rest of the structure down. The front door of the house was open and the broken windows on either side of the door gaped at the road.

"I hate to see that," Chrissie said.

"What?"

"An empty house. Every day when the bus comes by here I want to get off and shut the door. I wonder why they left the door open?"

"I couldn't tell you."

"What do you guess it would rent for?" she asked.

"I don't know. It would depend on how much land came with it."

"Do you think the house is still good?"

Jim looked in the rearview mirror, but the house was already out of sight around the curve behind them.

"I think it had a tin roof," he said. "The house should be okay if the roof's all right. Are you looking for a place to live?"

"We're staying with my grandparents until Daddy gets back from Oklahoma," she said. "Then we're going to need a bigger place."

"Who's 'we'?" Jim asked.

"Me and Mama."

"What's your daddy doing in Oklahoma?"

Chrissie kept looking out the window. "Working," she said.

They crossed Painter Creek a second time and drove into the long valley that lay between the creek and Lynn's Mountain. The valley was one of Jim's favorite places. The road wandered through prosperous-looking farms with painted houses and clean fencerows and thick green pastures. The soil in the creek bottoms was rich and brown. In the distance the mountain seemed to angle downward and disappear, along with the road, at some magic, unreachable point.

To the right of the road, a thick bank of white clouds had lowered itself onto the top two-thirds of the mountain. The bottom line of the clouds was so straight it could have been drawn with a ruler, and nothing about them suggested movement. They seemed to have come to stay.

When Jim leaned over to look through the passenger window, he smelled the vanilla extract Chrissie wore as perfume. He found himself in no hurry to sit up straight. She still held his handkerchief in her lap and hadn't unfolded it. He had never wanted to kiss anybody so badly in his whole life.

"Look at that," he said. "Most of the mountain's gone."

"I like it when it gets like that sometimes," Chrissie said. "Everything looks different and spooky, and it's like living somewhere else. Sometimes you just want to live somewhere else. But it gets old after a while. Have you ever lived on a mountain?"

"Nope. I've always been a town boy."

"I like living up high as long as I can see the sun," she said. "We used to live on a mountain up above Tuckaseegee, but we were on the wrong side."

"What do you mean, 'the wrong side'?"

"The side facing north. You don't ever want to live on the north side of a mountain. You don't get hardly any sun that way. The south side's always better."

"How long did you live there?"

"Four years. Then we moved to Oklahoma."

"How'd you like it?"

"Oklahoma or the mountain?"

"The mountain," Jim said.

"It was all right," Chrissie said. "It was pretty and green during the summer, but it felt like it started getting dark in the middle of the day and it seemed to rain constantly."

"The wrong side of the mountain," Jim said.

Chrissie nodded. "And you really had to look out for

copperheads. They were everywhere. One day Mama found one in the potato hole."

"What else?"

"Well, during the summer it seemed like mold would grow on your shoes overnight. And in the winter it was just awful. It never got light and the wind blew all the time and it stayed so cold you never could get your feet warm."

"Sounds like you didn't like it at all."

"That's not true," Chrissie said. "We just didn't have a good house. I intend to have a nice house someday." She looked at Jim seriously. "Y'all have nice houses, don't you?"

The question seemed to hold neither envy nor resentment, so Jim nodded.

"They look nice from the school."

"What about Oklahoma?" Jim asked.

"I didn't care for it. It didn't have any mountains that I saw, so it never looked right to me. You just get used to looking at mountains. Then, in the spring you had to worry about tornadoes, and it was way too hot in the summer." She shuddered a little. "And they have scorpions out there. You have to shake your shoes out before you put them on. I hate a scorpion worse than a snake."

"You never struck me as the kind of girl who would be afraid of anything."

"I never said I was afraid. I said I didn't like scorpions and snakes."

Jim grinned. "So, how was your house in Okla-homa?"

"We couldn't keep the dust out of it."

"I've never been out west," Jim said, "but I want to go someday."

Chrissie shrugged. "I don't think you're missing much. Some people like it, though."

They crested a short rise and the school bus Chrissie had missed materialized up ahead as if it had been conjured. It moved broadside to them at the spot where the road and creek turned in unison and raced toward the wooded side of the mountain.

"Do you want me to run the bus down for you?" Jim asked.

"No. Slow down. I can't let anybody see me in your car."

"Oh."

"That sounded awful, I know," Chrissie said. "But that's not how I meant it. Things are just kind of com-plicated right now."

"With Bucky Bucklaw?"

Chrissie tossed him a sharp look but didn't say anything.

"So, what do you want me to do?" Jim asked. "We're going to catch it pretty quick once it starts up the mountain."

"I don't know exactly. I guess we need to stop somewhere and wait," Chrissie said. "If that's all right with you."

Jim slowed the Major. "Do you want to turn around and go look at that old house?"

"That sounds good," Chrissie said.

Jim stopped the car in the yard and cut the engine. The house seemed to be trying to disappear into the landscape. It had once been painted white, but it had long since faded to a gray slightly darker than the color of the day; the roof had rusted to the red color of the muddy driveway. The open door and broken windows looked ominous.

"Who used to live here?" Chrissie asked.

"I don't remember their names," Jim said. "Some old couple. I saw them a few times from the road, but we never stopped. I guess they must have died."

"Oh," Chrissie said. "That's sad. And I guess they must not have had any kids to take over the place."

"I guess not."

"Do you think we ought to go in?"

"Why not?" Jim asked. "Are you scared?"

Chrissie stuck her tongue out at him. "No," she said. "I just didn't want to be disrespectful."

Beside the house stood a black walnut tree already devoid of leaves, save for a few yellow stragglers clinging to the topmost branches. The upstairs window of the house was open to the weather, and one of the tree's limbs reached through it as if feeling around for the lock. Jim imagined that the house, or someone or something inside it, was listening to them as they approached, and he caught himself stepping through the weeds as quietly as possible, almost tiptoeing. He stopped on the top step and checked the soundness of the porch before venturing onto it. When Chrissie stepped onto the porch behind him, the boards creaked deliciously, and he felt gooseflesh scamper up his arms.

When he turned and looked at Chrissie, her eyes had warmed with excitement into some miraculous, glowing shade of brown, a color Jim had never seen before. For a moment he couldn't remember how to move his legs. He felt himself smile so broadly, so ridiculously, that he would not have been surprised had sunshine poured out of his mouth.

"What?" Chrissie asked.

"You look scared," Jim said.

"No, I don't."

Jim smiled again. "You're right. You don't."

The delicate segments of her irises seemed to have been cut from some impossibly fine glass, except that, as Chrissie's pupils widened in the shaded light of the porch, they changed shape while he studied them.

"Why are you staring at me?" Chrissie asked. "You look like a possum. All that grinning."

Jim pretended to take offense. "A possum," he said. "I don't look like a possum."

Chrissie giggled. "You're right," she said. "You don't."

At the threshold Jim pushed against the door, but

it had swollen into place against the floorboards. He stepped sideways through the opening into a dim, unpainted hallway that bisected the length of the house and stopped at what Jim guessed was the back door. On the right side of the hallway a stairway disappeared up into the shadows, and beyond the stairway stood a single doorway; on the left side two doors faced the hall. The shadows between Jim and the exit at the back of the house seemed to possess mass and bones; had Jim been a few years younger, he would have turned around and run as fast as he could. Chrissie stepped into the house behind him. She grasped the doorknob and pulled but could only move it two or three inches. The doorsill scraping against the floor of the silent house struck Jim as one of the loudest noises he had ever heard.

"What are you doing?" he asked. He noticed that he was whispering, so he forced himself to loudly repeat the question. He still thought he sounded scared.

"Houses know when people don't live in them," she said. "Did you ever notice that?"

"What?"

"Look at this door. It's rotten and it's all swelled up."

"I guess it got wet," Jim said. He checked the ceiling for water stains but didn't find any.

"It knows that nobody lives here anymore so it started rotting."

"That's crazy," Jim said.

Chrissie scowled at him impatiently. "Have you ever seen an old house that had fallen in?"

"Sure. Lots of times. So?"

"Well, have you ever seen a house that fell in while somebody was still living in it?"

Jim thought for a minute. "No. I guess not."

"Then, you tell me what that proves."

"I don't know what that proves."

"Yes, you do," Chrissie said.

She stepped past him toward the door opposite the stairway, which opened into what must have been the house's parlor. The walls of the room had once been papered with an old-fashioned pattern of pink roses on a pale background, but large strips of the paper had been ripped from the walls and now lay twisted about the floor. The shredded wallpaper shared the floor with the broken glass from the windows and the rocks that had broken them. The glass crunched underneath their feet. Jim kicked one of the rocks and it fled noisily into a corner. He looked through the windows and saw the Major obediently watching the house. He noticed that neither of them had shut their door all the way.

Chrissie found an old broom leaning in the corner and took a couple of halfhearted swipes at the floor. She called to Jim from across the room. "Look at the fireplace," she said.

"Somebody pulled up the hearth."

"Whoever it was, they were looking for money. I bet that poor couple wasn't even cold in the grave before somebody broke in here looking for their savings. Don't you think people are just awful?"

"We're in here," Jim said.

"But we don't have bad intentions."

He walked over and looked into the hole where the hearth had been but saw only the ground underneath the house. The hearthstone lay off to one side. It was a large piece of fieldstone that someone had roughly chiseled into shape. Jim studied it for a moment, then worked his fingers underneath it and slid it back into place.

"There," he said.

"Thank you," said Chrissie.

She squatted and ran her finger around the edge of a perfectly round hole, about the size of a silver dollar, cut into one corner of the hearth. "What do you guess this was for?"

Jim suddenly brightened with the answer. "Walnuts," he said. "There's a big walnut tree in the front yard. They used to put the walnuts into the hole and bust them open with a hammer."

Chrissie snapped her fingers. "That's it," she said. "That's it exactly. They sat here by the fire in the wintertime and shelled walnuts. Whose job do you think it was?"

"His," Jim said.

"Then she would put them into pound cakes."

"Whatever was left over. He ate most of them out of the shell."

"Well, then, I hope he was ashamed."

"He was."

When they left the parlor they tiptoed down the hallway, and Jim pushed open the door of the room on the right. The floor was covered in trash, with chicken bones and empty whiskey bottles and torn magazines and piles of old clothing; a man's single shoe, rotting and curled up at the toe, lay on a soiled mattress in the corner. The ticking of the mattress was almost entirely blackened by dark stains.

"Tramps," Jim said. "Tramps stay here." He thought about going to get his rifle out of the Major.

"Lost people," Chrissie said. "Lost people stay here. Just because somebody is lost doesn't mean you have to call them a tramp."

She moved past him into the room and with the handle of the old broom poked through the piles of trash.

"Are you looking for something in particular?" Jim asked.

"No. I'm just looking."

When she reached the mattress she stood staring down at it a long time. She jabbed at the shoe with the broom. When she turned around, Jim thought she looked a little scared.

"I have a bad feeling about this room," she said. "Bad things have happened here."

"Then, let's go."

Chrissie dropped the broom and tiptoed quickly across the floor. Jim shut the door securely behind her. He watched her carefully. If she had run for the car, he would have run, too.

"Say a prayer," she said.

"What?"

"Say a prayer. There are bad spirits in there and we don't want them to follow us when we leave."

"What kind of spirits?"

"Spirits of despair," Chrissie said. "Say a prayer to protect us."

"You say one."

"I'm going to say one for the lost people. You say one about the spirits."

Jim closed his eyes. At first he couldn't think of anything to pray, but then the words *Lord, in the coming months protect us all from the spirits of despair* whispered into his mind. The words puzzled and frightened him a little, and he tried to shake them out of his head. He never said them out loud. When he opened his eyes he saw Chrissie studying him.

"Amen," she said.

"Amen."

"Do you think we're safe here?"

Jim closed his eyes again and listened but heard only the silence of the empty rooms and the slightly urgent sound of his own breathing. "I think we're okay," he said. "I don't think there's anybody else in here. Are the spirits after us?"

"Not right now," she said.

Across the hallway they found the room that had

once been the kitchen. A black stovepipe poked out of the wall, and beneath the stovepipe lay a sooty tin fire mat. Jim studied the four deep indentations in the tin and pictured a fat stove squatting there, connected to the chimney by the pipe, a fire burning in the box, a pound cake with walnuts cooking in the oven; the fact that a stove no longer occupied the place where a stove so obviously belonged made the room seem strangely forlorn. An overturned wooden chair lay on each side of the fire mat. The strips of oak caning the bottoms of the chairs were busted downward. Someone had apparently forced a foot through each of the seats.

"Their chairs," Chrissie said. "They liked to sit by the stove."

She righted one of the chairs and perched primly on the edge of the broken seat. She pointed with her chin at the other chair. "You sit there," she said.

Jim picked up the chair and turned it so that its back faced Chrissie; he squatted across the seat and sat on the frame. He draped his arms across the back, and Mama would ask him later how he had gotten his shirt so dirty.

Chrissie watched him a long time, the look on her face unreadable. Then she dropped her chin to her chest and frowned.

"What did I do?" Jim asked.

"Old man," she said, "I can't believe you ate all the walnuts."

Jim blinked rapidly, then smiled. Once again he

felt sunshine pouring out of his mouth. "Old woman," he said in a gruff voice, "I didn't eat *all* the walnuts. I just ate *most* of the walnuts."

"You didn't leave me enough to make a cake."

"Well, I don't know what you expect me to do about it now. You know I flat love walnuts."

"I think you're a very selfish old man."

"Am I?"

Chrissie slowly nodded. "You only think about what you want. You never, ever think about what I want."

"But they were just walnuts."

"Not to me," she said.

"Chrissie . . ."

She started, or pretended to. "What did you call me, old man?"

"Ah," he said. "Old woman, I'm afraid I'm getting forgetful in my old age. Tell me, what did you say your name was?"

"Juanita Loretta Rebecca," she said.

"And what's my name again?"

She closed one eye, cocked her head, and carefully considered him. "Hernando Amos Grover," she said.

Jim laughed out loud. "Okay, then," he said. "If old Hernando Amos Grover goes and shells you some more walnuts, will you forgive him?"

Chrissie stared at him sadly. "Probably," she said. "I always do."

At that moment, whatever reserve and decorum that had held Jim in his chair, that for weeks had kept him from telling Chrissie how he felt, that had kept him from swimming to Hawaii and challenging Bucky Bucklaw to a fistfight, simply went away. He stood up and moved around the fire mat and knelt on one knee in front of Chrissie. Reaching into her lap, he picked up her right hand. He turned it palm upward and studied it the way he might have studied some book whose pages contained everything he needed to know in writing too small to read. When she didn't withdraw her hand, he placed it against his cheek. Now it was warm and dry and smooth. Jim closed his eyes. He felt on the verge of calamity, and he had never felt more wonderful in his life. When he opened his eyes and spoke, his voice shook and came out lower than he had ever heard it. "Juanita," he said, "you're the best thing that ever happened to me. I don't know what I would do without you."

"You're a crazy old man," she said softly, "saying a thing like that. If something happened to me, you know you'd just go off and marry somebody else."

"No," he said. "I would never do that."

"You would, too. You just love me for my pound cakes."

"That's not true," Jim said. "I love everything about you."

Chrissie withdrew her hand. One strong feeling after another moved silently across her face like the shadows cast by clouds. One moment she looked fierce, and the next she looked ready to kiss him, and the next she looked as sad as anyone he had ever seen. Jim couldn't tell from instant to instant what she might be thinking, so he didn't dare move. He had the distinct feeling that whatever was about to happen would be the first really important thing to happen to him in his entire life. Chrissie might tell him she loved him, and she might punch him in the eye. Either way, Jim was sure that the boy who left this kitchen would be an entirely different boy than the one who had entered it.

"Jim . . . ," she said softly.

"Shh," he said. "Hernando. Please call me Hernando."

Chrissie reached out with a finger, as if to brush the hair away from his forehead, but seemed to think better of it and dropped her hand into her lap.

"Jim," she said, "I think we need to get on up the road."

"Chrissie, can I kiss you?"

He watched as her chin first moved almost imperceptibly to the right, and then farther, with more assurance, to the left and back again.

"No," she said. "You can't."

Jim and the Beanstalk

ABOUT A third of the way up the mountain, the world disappeared. One minute Jim and Chrissie were traveling upward along a path Chrissie knew well and Jim knew somewhat: through open, second-growth stands of oak and maple and poplar and sweet gum muted by the drizzle and gathering fog; through rich hells of laurel and rhododendron, out of which carried the tumbling voices of creek branches and wet-weather springs too small for names; up slopes too steep for logging, where ancient pine trees of impossible girth and height still climbed out of sight. But the next minute, the cloud they had seen from the valley silently closed around them, and every landmark — every rock, bush, tree, and opening in the trees, every mud hole, bank, ditch, straightaway, and switchback — that marked the mountain as a place recognizable to them simply ceased to be. Jim slowed the Major and downshifted into first; he leaned forward until his chest touched the steering wheel, but he could see no more than a car length of road at a time unrolling ahead of them. For all he could tell, a car length of road was all that lay between them and falling off the edge of the world into the void feared long ago by sailors. He switched on the headlights, but the enveloping whiteness swallowed the feeble light the Major manufactured as easily as it had swallowed everything else. The windshield wipers also proved to be of little use. Jim felt a panicky sweat blossom in his armpits.

"I don't know about you," he said, "but I can't see a daggum thing."

Chrissie, too, leaned forward and squinted into the fog. "I can't see anything, either," she said. "You be careful."

"I'm going to."

They had talked little since leaving the abandoned house. Jim was still tormented by a desire to kiss Chrissie — for that matter, by an overwhelming, though still somewhat vague, longing to *possess* her in general — but surprisingly did not feel awkward riding in the car with her. Likewise, Chrissie seemed to find traveling up the mountain with Jim a perfectly pleasant way to pass the time. Though she had refused to kiss him, she had, however briefly, pretended to be married to him; that make-believe intimacy, and the make-believe years on which it was built, seemed to remain comfortably settled around their shoulders — even as they left Hernando and Juanita sitting in their broken chairs by their ghostly stove, forever arguing about walnuts.

"I've never been inside a cloud before," Jim said. "How about you?"

"Nothing like this. I've never seen anything like this in my life."

As long as Jim drove no faster than he could have walked, road enough to navigate continued to materialize before them. The switchbacks, however, proved to be especially frightening because Jim had to speed up in order to climb through them without stalling. But when he accelerated, waves of fog leapt angrily at the windshield and crashed against the glass, and the edge of the earth hurtled forward just inches ahead of the car's front tires. Eventually Jim began to feel disoriented and dizzy. The Major seemed balanced on top of a flagpole, or caught in the uppermost branches of a tree; Jim was afraid that the slightest misstep on his part would send them plummeting into space. He kept driving, but his neck and shoulders ached with tension.

When the switchbacks stopped rolling at them and Jim felt the road level out, he knew that they had driven out into the high, narrow valley that lay beneath the ridgeline of the mountain. A mailbox sprang into being suddenly on the right, and Jim had to swerve to miss it. More mailboxes, sometimes whole rows of them, appeared then at regular intervals, like sentries at the ends of the narrow, rutted roads that spilled down out of the deep hollows that creased the side of the ridge. And when the road rose again, Jim knew that they had reached the end of the valley, and that beside them, below the road, lay the bald from which — on a clear day — it was possible to see not only Aliceville but, farther away, the brick cotton mills that straddled the river at Roberta and Allendale and, beyond the mills, the hazy, patchwork country rolling away until at some point it mysteriously became South Carolina. Jim could feel the great empty space yawning to his left, although he could not see it, and the knowledge that it lay only yards away from where he drove made his heart leap like he had just dreamed he was falling. He stopped the car.

"Let's get out here for a minute," he said.

He climbed out but kept a hand safely on the reassuring bulk of the car. Chrissie walked around the Major and stood beside him — at a companionable distance, he thought, but not nearly close enough — and together they stared into the fog and imagined the world that lay beyond it.

"Look," Jim said. "You can see my house from here."

"I know."

"You mean you've looked for it?"

"I mean you can see a long way from here. And I mean I've seen your house."

Jim nodded. The air was perfectly still, but the fog was chilly on his face. He shivered and stuck his hands in his pockets. He didn't know what else to say. Hoping that Chrissie had viewed his house as more important than any other house visible from the mountain had been too much to hope for.

"I know what," Chrissie said. "Let's be really quiet and see if we can hear anything."

Jim let go of the Major and stood up straight. He cocked his ear toward the place where he knew the mountain fell away into the air. He closed his eyes, but that made him feel like he was falling, so he opened them again. Dead silence. He couldn't remember ever being anyplace where he couldn't hear anything at all. No wind blowing or dogs barking in the distance or Mama moving around in the next room or the low murmur of the uncles talking as they rocked on the porch. Nothing. He and Chrissie could have been the only living things left on earth, an idea that made him as happy as he could remember ever being — despite the fact that the noises that came to mind had always made him happy before. Eventually Chrissie took a deep breath and exhaled.

"I couldn't hear anything," Jim said. "Could you?"

"Nope," she said. "I feel like we just climbed the beanstalk."

Jim smiled. "You never know. Maybe we did."

"Now all we have to worry about is getting past the giant's house."

"Do you think he'd kill us if he knew we were up here?"

"More than likely," she said. "And then I think he'd eat us."

"I ain't afraid of no giant," Jim said. "I'll chop his head off if he messes with us."

"Well, *I'm* still glad it's foggy," Chrissie said. "You never know when he's watching. I'm going to walk up the road and count my footsteps, and you tell me when you can't see me anymore."

"You're not going to run off, are you?"

"Not right now. Just tell me when you can't see me."

Jim watched Chrissie walk off into the fog and listened to her counting slowly. By the time she counted to five, her outline began to grow indistinct, and by the time she reached twenty, she vanished entirely. The last thing Jim saw fade out of sight was the long, black stripe of her hair.

"There," he said.

"You can't see me anymore?"

"No. Can you see me?"

"There's sort of a dark place where your car's parked, but I can't tell what it is."

Jim squinted at the spot where he had last seen Chrissie and rubbed the gooseflesh on his arms. He felt suddenly heartbroken, and wished she would come back.

"Are you still there?" he asked.

"I'm still here."

"You looked like a ghost," he said. "You just disappeared."

"I feel like a ghost. Are you sure you can't see me?"

"I'm sure."

"Then you can ask me three questions."

"What?"

"You get to ask three questions when you climb the beanstalk. But only if you can't see the person you're asking."

"I've never heard that part of the story," he said.

"You just didn't have the right person telling it," she answered.

"Three questions aren't enough."

"But that's the way this story goes."

"Okay. Let me think."

"Number one."

"All right," he said. "Here goes. Number one. Are you an Indian?"

"Half," she said. "I can't believe you wasted a question on that. Number two."

"Number two. Do you get sick like that every month?"

Chrissie didn't say anything at first. "Yes," she said finally. "But only since we moved back to North Carolina, and only for a few hours at a time, and only on the first day."

"That's awful."

"I'll live. These aren't very good questions, Jim."

"I'll try to do better."

"Okay. Number three."

"Number three. Are you Bucky Bucklaw's girl-friend?"

"That's complicated."

"What do you mean 'complicated'?"

"That's four questions, Jim."

"Then answer number three."

"I don't know how to answer number three."

"It seems easy enough to me," Jim said.

"Well, it's not."

"Either you're going with Bucky Bucklaw or you're not going with Bucky Bucklaw. Which one is it?"

Somewhere up the road he heard Chrissie stomp her foot.

"Look here, Jim, I can't be your girlfriend," she said. "All right?"

"Nobody asked you to be my girlfriend," Jim said. "But why not?"

"That's five."

"Damn it, Chrissie," Jim said. "Will you please, please, please stop counting?"

"No more questions, Jim."

"But you didn't tell me what I need to know."

"Take me home," she said.

"I'm not taking you home until you answer number three."

"When you take me home, you'll know the answer to number three."

The road wound through the half dozen buildings clustered in the small village of Lynn's Mountain, though all Jim saw of it was the store and a handful of tombstones in the graveyard at the church. Chrissie pointed at the tombstones and smiled as they passed but did so without comment. Jim was pleased that they had apparently just shared something, even though he didn't know what it was.

"You can ask me questions if you want to," he said. "You climbed the beanstalk, too."

"How many questions?"

"As many as you want. I'm not stingy like some people I know."

"Why did you break up with Norma Harris?" Chrissie asked.

Jim winced and twisted in his seat. "I don't know," he said. "It just wasn't any fun, I guess. That's the main reason. Is that a bad reason?"

"I don't know if it is or not. Y'all seem like you belong together. You're both fair-skinned and your hair's the same color. You're both real smart and you seem a little stuck-up at first."

"Well, we don't belong together, and I'm not stuck up. Ask me another question."

"Why do you want to be my boyfriend?"

"What makes you think I want to be your boyfriend?"

"I'm not stupid, Jim," she said. "You play with my hair during history class. You stare at me all the time. And you came to give me a ride when you heard I was sick. That was a very nice thing to do, by the way."

"Thank you," he said. "You can feel it when I touch your hair?"

"It's attached to my head," she said. "Of course I can feel it. But you didn't answer me. Why do you want to be my boyfriend?"

Jim gripped the steering wheel tighter. Chrissie had

finally asked the question; he was going to step up and answer it truthfully, Bucky Bucklaw be damned.

"Because I love you," he said.

"Oh," she said, looking down into her lap. "I see."

"I've loved you since you got off the bus the first day of school."

"Now, wait a minute. That just sounds like something that boys say to girls."

"Well, maybe it was the second day."

"That's better."

"And I know I don't know you very well," Jim said. "So, you don't have to tell me that. I don't understand it, either."

"I wasn't going to say that. I think we at least ought to be able to love whoever we want to, even if it's not a good idea."

"Well, at least that's one thing we agree on, I guess."

That seemed to be the end of it. Jim had always imagined that telling Chrissie he loved her would lead to more discussion, but then again, he couldn't remember talking about love much with Norma, either. Maybe love was just one of those things it didn't take long to talk about.

Close by the roadside, a mountain of logs marked the yard of Carson's Mill, and from out of the fog they heard the banshee keening of the big saw blade. Jim noticed that Chrissie shivered at the sound. A little farther up the road he tried to see his friend Penn's house but couldn't find even the mailbox.

"Where does that Carson boy go to boarding school again?" Chrissie asked.

"Outside Philadelphia somewhere."

"I saw him around a time or two over the summer. He's handsome."

"He's got that bad limp, though," Jim said.

"That's not a very nice thing to say about somebody who's had polio. Especially when they're supposed to be your friend."

"You're right. I don't know why I said it."

"Yes, you do."

"Is there anything else you want to ask me?" Jim said.

"Did you know that my mama and your uncle Zeno almost got married?"

"What?" he said. *"What?"*

"They broke it off at the last minute."

"I never heard anything about Uncle Zeno even having a girlfriend, much less one he almost married. Why did they break up?"

"I don't know," Chrissie said. "Mama won't talk about it. She says it's ancient history."

"So Uncle Zeno had a girlfriend," Jim said. "My, my, my. Is your mama pretty?"

Chrissie briefly looked upward, studying some picture Jim couldn't see. "I don't know anymore," she said. "I guess she was at one time. Does it matter?"

"No. I guess not."

He drove through the ford on Painter Creek and crept the Major past the spot where his grandfather's house had stood. Jim had visited the old man only once before he died. In the fog there was nothing to see — the house had fallen in several years before — and nothing to hear, but Jim still felt uneasy passing by it. He pointed out the window.

"That's where my grandfather's house used to be," he said.

"You can still see the chimney from the road," Chrissie said. "It always gives me a bad feeling."

"You get bad feelings about a lot of things."

"There's a lot in the world to feel bad about."

"I guess I never thought that way," Jim said. "I think there's a lot in the world to feel good about."

"I heard your grandfather bought your grandmother from her daddy and treated her real bad. Isn't that enough to give somebody a bad feeling when they see his old chimney sticking up?"

Jim accelerated the Major slightly. "I didn't have anything to do with it," he said.

A mile or so past Amos Glass's place, the road switchbacked twice in rapid succession, then straightened out and continued upward toward the far western reach of the mountain. Soon they drove out into the apple orchards owned by Bucky Bucklaw's father, Arthur Bucklaw Sr. Save for the few apple trees crouched close to the road, Jim could not have said how he knew that they had driven out into open country; he knew only that they had.

"You turn to the right up here," Chrissie said.

"You *live* on the Bucklaw place?" Jim said.

"Yep."

"I didn't know that. I thought you lived just past it somewhere."

"Nope. We live on it."

"Huh."

"But it's only until my daddy gets here."

"When's that going to be?"

"I'm not sure."

Arthur Bucklaw Sr. had moved with his wife from the Casar side of the mountain to the Aliceville side thirty years earlier, where, much to the amusement of his neighbors, he purchased five adjoining farmsteads of almost unworkable steepness and immediately went to work setting out fruit trees. The sunny, southern slope of the mountain had proved ideal for growing apples, however, and Bucklaw Sr. had made what everyone agreed must have been a great deal of money, and this despite the Depression. Many of the people who had laughed at him now picked apples for him in the fall. The responsibility for rubbing people's noses in just how much money Bucklaw had made seemed to have fallen to his only son, Bucky. Jim thought that the uncles were probably worth more than the Bucklaws, but he had no way of knowing for sure. At least with Bucky graduated out of high school and off the baseball team and gone away to the navy, he didn't have to think about it so often.

After Jim turned off the main road onto the Bucklaw place, he drove down a narrow boulevard of huge packing sheds and barns that grew one at a time out of the fog like the palaces and temples of a ghostly city. He assumed they had been built, in typical Bucklaw fashion, within spitting distance of the road simply so they wouldn't be missed by visitors. Despite the hearty contempt Jim held for Bucky, the closer they drew to the Bucklaw house, the more nervous he became. Chrissie, likewise, slumped down in her seat, hiding from any Bucklaw who might magically be able to see her slinking past. The house, which occupied the top of a small knoll set back from the drive, was at least mercifully obscured by the fog.

"Slow down," Chrissie said. "You don't want to run over those dogs."

Jim had opened his mouth to say "What dogs?" when he suddenly found himself face-to-face with a nightmare constructed of sharp claws, large teeth, and hateful, pale eyes — two wolflike dogs who threw themselves at his window, apparently trying to chew through the glass. After a few horrifying seconds, the dogs vanished just as quickly as they had appeared, leaving behind an impressive layer of dog slobber and muddy paw prints on his window.

"Good Lord," he said. "What in the world was that?"

"Bucky's dogs," Chrissie said. "They're German shepherds."

"I'm glad I had the window rolled up."

"I would've warned you if you hadn't. They might've gotten in here and chewed you all to pieces."

"What about you?"

"Oh, they know me."

At Chrissie's direction, Jim pulled into a muddy clearing walled off by a thicket of scruffy-looking pines. He parked beside a decrepit Model T truck whose flatbed was constructed of mismatched lumber.

"We're here," she said.

When Jim cut the engine, he heard what sounded like an immense pack of hounds baying urgently somewhere close by. In the fog the noise seemed to come from all directions at once. He expected to see more vicious dogs, hundreds of them this time, loping out of the trees. He hesitated before getting out.

"What about those dogs?" he asked. "Are they going to chew me all to pieces?"

"They're penned up," Chrissie said, shutting her door.

"What are they?"

"Plotts mostly. Some blueticks. Mr. Bucklaw uses them to hunt bears."

"Bear dogs," Jim said. The uncles used their hounds to hunt raccoons. "How many does he have?"

"I don't know. Twenty or twenty-five, I guess. You're not allowed to pet them because they're bear dogs, so I don't pay them any mind. They smell bad, too. My paw-paw takes care of them for Mr. Bucklaw."

She led him up a narrow path into the pines. The dogs' voices ran in and out of the fog; they surged forward and retreated from every direction he turned. The baying grew louder and more urgent the farther he and Chrissie walked. He squinted up the path.

"Are you sure they're penned up?" he asked.

Chrissie smiled and took his hand. "Don't worry, Jim. I won't let them get you."

Up ahead he heard a door creak open. A man's voice yelled, "Hey! You there!" and the dogs fell silent on a single note. The door creaked closed.

"That's Paw-paw," Chrissie said.

They walked into another clearing and a house began to form itself out of the fog. It seemed to be misshapen at first — the house in a children's story where a troll might live — but eventually it sharpened into a dogtrot cabin whose sagging ridgepole dipped toward a covered passageway separating two log rooms. Chimneys of rough fieldstones plastered with mud rose unsteadily on either side of the house, just high enough to clear the roof. The roof was covered by ancient wooden shingles, patched here and there with flattened tin cans. Jim could see tiny slivers of light leaking from in between the logs of the walls. In the places where the chinking had fallen away entirely, someone had stuffed wads of old newsprint into the cracks.

A single hound Jim couldn't locate barked a sharp warning, and a door on the left front of the cabin swung open. A feeble column of orange kerosene light tipped across the yard, and the silhouetted shape of a stooped old man appeared in the doorway. The old man had only one arm; his right sleeve dangled emptily by his side.

"Who's out there?" he demanded.

Chrissie dropped Jim's hand as they stepped into the light. "It's me, Paw-paw," she said.

Jim had never known that Chrissie's family was as poor as this house revealed them to be; he felt immensely sad that she had to live in such a place, and he took an immediate, irrational dislike to the old man who stood before them. He needed to blame Chrissie's predicament on someone, and the old man was the only possibility to present itself so far.

"Where you been, girl?"

"I got sick at school. I missed the bus and had to get a ride home."

"Who's that with you?"

"This is Jim Glass," she said. "He's the one who gave me the ride."

"Jim Glass," the old man said. "I knew your grand-daddy."

"Yes, sir."

"He was a bastard."

"Paw-paw," Chrissie said.

"Well, he was. No reason not to call a spade a spade."

Jim almost smiled. Amos Glass had been a bastard, but to Jim's knowledge nobody ever called him one until after he died.

"Jim, this is my paw-paw, Solon McAbee," Chrissie said.

"Nub," Mr. McAbee said.

"Excuse me?" Jim said.

"Everybody calls me Nub."

"Oh. Nice to meet you, sir."

"I can see you're wondering what happened to my arm."

"Oh, no, sir," Jim said.

"Paw-paw, you always do this," Chrissie complained.

"I wore it off playing the fiddle, is what happened," Mr. McAbee said. He opened the door wider and stepped to one side. "Y'all get on in here. You're letting all the fog in."

"This is the only time I'll ever be able to bring you up here," Chrissie whispered. "Look at everything close and you'll know the answer to number three."

Once inside, Jim studied the room intently. In the center of the floor the old man drew a chair from underneath a homemade table covered with an oil-cloth and sat down. The wide pine planks of the floor had been worn thin and splintery, but they were swept clean. The walls were sealed with newspapers and pieces of cardboard tacked up by nails driven through old bottle caps. A large, rusting cookstove dominated the wall facing the door, and a black pot of greens bubbled on the stove. To the right, a small bed, made neatly with a worn but clean feed-sack quilt, lay along the wall beside a misshapen door Jim assumed opened into the dogtrot. A teddy bear slumped against the wall and stared into the room as if he could not believe his misfortune. On the left, two women sat on either side of the fireplace, although no fire had been lit inside it. One woman was old and shriveled and as dry-looking as an old harness. She had no teeth and her white hair was pulled back into a painful-looking bun. The other looked like an older, tired version of Chrissie, although her hair was brown, going to gray, and not black.

"Who's that with you?" the younger woman asked.

"Mama, this is Jim Glass," Chrissie said. "I got sick again at school and he gave me a ride home. Jim, that's my mama, Nancy Steppe."

"Hello, Mrs. Steppe," Jim said. "Pleased to meet you."

Mrs. Steppe nodded to him, expressionless, but didn't take her eyes off his face.

The older woman leaned over, picked up a tin can from the hearth, and spat into it. "Did anybody see you drive up in here?"

"Jim, that's my grandmother, Effie McAbee."

"Hello," Jim said.

The old woman nodded curtly at Jim and spat into the can again. Jim disliked her as instinctively as he had disliked the old man. She had the bright, appraising eyes of a small dog plotting to steal food from a bigger dog.

"The fog sure is thick out there today," Jim said to the old woman. "Nobody can see much of anything."

"It ain't that thick," Mrs. McAbee said.

"I knew your family, a long time ago," Mrs. Steppe said. "I trust everybody's doing well."

"Yes, ma'am," Jim said. "Thank you. Everybody's fine, about the same, I guess."

"Business doing good, I hope?"

Jim felt his face tighten. He had learned from the uncles a long time ago never to discuss the family businesses with anyone outside the family.

"We're doing all right," he said. "Things seem to be picking up."

"Picking up," mumbled the old woman.

"That's good," Mrs. Steppe said. "I imagine they must be awfully worried about you, driving around up here in all this fog. You should probably head on back. It'll be dark before you make it down the mountain."

Jim backed up a step. "Oh. Yes, ma'am. I guess I ought to be going."

"I'll walk you to your car," said Chrissie.

"Well," Jim said. "It was nice to meet y'all."

The old woman stared at him with her bright eyes. "Don't run off," she said.

"I need to get on."

Chrissie's mother's smile suggested she remembered something funny that had nothing to do with the current conversation. "You tell your people Nancy McAbee asked about them," she said.

"Steppe," said Chrissie.

"I'll do that."

"And, boy," said Mr. McAbee. "Whatever you do, don't let 'em make you take up the fiddle."

"I won't," Jim said. "Well, bye."

"Don't run over them dogs," the old woman said.

"I won't. I'll be careful. Y'all take care."

Chrissie took Jim by the arm and steered him toward the door. When he stepped outside he heard the old woman say, "If he runs over them dogs, there'll be a world of trouble."

"Hush, Mama," Chrissie's mother said. "He'll hear you."

Walking back to the car, Chrissie held on to Jim's arm with both hands. Her clinging to him didn't make him happy, however, because he could tell that she was unhappy.

"Hey," he said. "What's the matter?"

"Now do you know the answer to number three?" she asked.

"I'm not sure. Maybe. I think so."

"Then, tell me what you think it is."

"No. You tell me."

"All right," Chrissie said. "Number three. You see where we live."

Jim nodded.

"And you know who owns it."

"Bucky's daddy."

"Right. So, when me and Mama moved back here, Bucky just up and decided on his own that I was his private property. Before he went off to the navy, he told everybody up here I was his girlfriend. Now nobody else is allowed to talk to me."

"And you just let him?"

She let go and stepped away from him. "You're not thinking, Jim," she said. "My paw-paw's only got one arm."

"So?"

"So, what if I make Bucky mad and Mr. Bucklaw runs us off? What do you think would happen then?"

"I don't know."

"I'll tell you what would happen. We wouldn't have any place to live, and we wouldn't have any money, and nobody would hire my paw-paw because he's dead old and was stupid enough to get his stupid arm cut off in the sawmill, and then we'd be up the creek so far nobody would ever find us. We're poor as church mice as it is."

"You can't let them get away with that," Jim said. "You can't let Bucky do that to you."

"I don't have any choice in it."

"What do you mean you don't have any choice?"

"I mean that people with money can do just about anything they want to people who don't have money."

"That's not true. I don't believe that."

"You've always had money."

"You wait just a minute," Jim said. "My family's not rich, and nobody ever gave us anything. We've worked for everything we've got."

"How many houses does your family own?" Chrissie asked.

Jim didn't answer.

"How many?"

"Three," he said, "not counting the tenant house, but it's falling in."

"Three houses. And how many people live in those three houses?"

"Five."

"Five people in three houses," Chrissie said. "So, let me tell you something. I sleep in a *kitchen,* so don't you dare tell me you're not rich. *My* family doesn't have a pot to pee in, and I don't know where my daddy is or when he's coming to get us, and Mr. Bucklaw watches me like a hawk, and my mattress is made out of corn shucks and I can hear bugs crawling around in it, and then you drive up here in your dumb car with its dumb name like some kind of big shot and talk to me like I'm stupid and say, '*Oh, I'm not rich,*' and tell me that I can just break up with Bucky Bucklaw pretty as you please?"

Jim stopped walking. "Whoa," he said. "I'm sorry. Please don't cry. I just wasn't thinking."

When he reached out and tried to take Chrissie by the arms, she slapped his hands away. "Don't touch me," she said.

"Shh," Jim said.

"I mean it, Jim Glass. You can't put your hands on me just so it'll make you feel better. If you ever touch me again, I swear to God I'll knock those nice straight teeth of yours right down your throat."

"Listen to me."

"Don't you dare touch me. I'll kill you if you touch me."

"I won't touch you. I promise. Just listen."

Chrissie glared at him. "What?" she said.

Jim took a deep breath.

"I'm just sorry," he said. "I'm really, really sorry. I don't know anything about your life . . ."

"That's right, you don't."

"And I'm sorry if I acted like I did."

"Okay."

"And I'm sorry Bucky has got you so jammed up, and I'm sorry you don't have a nice house, because you deserve one, and I'm sorry you have a corn-shuck bed, and I'm sorry you got sick today, and I'm just awful sorry about everything, and I would change it all if I could so you wouldn't have to be sad ever again, because I love you."

Chrissie blinked, nodded curtly, turned, and continued down the path.

Jim fell into step beside her. "Why don't you ever say anything when I tell you that I love you?" he asked. "I've been telling you that all afternoon."

"I heard you," Chrissie said without looking at him, "and I think you're a very nice boy. But I also think you've never learned you don't get to have everything you want every time you want it."

"You make me sound like Bucky Bucklaw."

Chrissie shrugged. "You are like Bucky Bucklaw."

"I don't think that's fair."

"It's just the truth."

"Are you in love with him?"

"No," Chrissie said. "There's your car."

When Jim opened the door he noticed for the first time that the light was failing. It would be dark soon and he was a long way from home. Mama would be worried sick.

"Are you in love with me?"

Chrissie shook her head angrily. "Jim. Listen to me. If I lived somewhere else and had some different kind of life, I could lay around all day on my pretty bed and think about which boy I loved and which boy I didn't and then I'd dress up all pretty and write about it in my diary. But I don't live somewhere else, and this life is the only one I've got. I don't have time to think about things like that."

Jim slid underneath the wheel, slammed the door, and rolled down the window. "Have you kissed Bucky Bucklaw?" he asked.

"You're asking way too many questions."

"I'm not going to get mad. I just need to know."

"Bucky's kissed me," she said. "But I haven't kissed Bucky."

"What's the difference?"

"There's a difference."

"Oh."

"Do you know what I mean?"

"No."

Chrissie leaned in through the car window and kissed Jim so quickly on the lips he didn't have time to shut his eyes.

"Hey, wait a minute," he said. "I wasn't ready. Let me kiss you again."

She shook her head and backed away from the car. "Have a nice trip," she said.

*   *   *

Jim rolled up his window and drove carefully as he approached the Bucklaw house. He figured the dogs would be waiting for him to come back by and he didn't want to run over one of them, no matter how much he thought it was a good idea. He was still searching for the dogs, his heart racing, when the fog to his left began to brighten. The brightening condensed into the circular glow of a lantern, and as he drew closer, the form of a very tall man squeezed into being out of the light. Two large dogs sat on either side of the man, their bushy tails curled around their haunches. The man held up a hand as Jim approached; when Jim stopped the car, he tapped on the glass. Jim looked into the amber eyes of the panting dogs and rolled the window down less than halfway. The man leaned slowly over, held the lantern up, and looked into the car.

"Hey, Mr. Bucklaw," Jim said. "It's me, Jim Glass. I played baseball with Bucky."

"I know who you are," Arthur Bucklaw said. "What are you doing up in here?"

"Christine Steppe got sick at school today and missed the bus, so I gave her a ride home."

"You running a taxi service, then?"

"No, sir."

"Then how come you're driving a taxi?"

"I'm not driving a taxi. I just gave Chrissie a ride."

The upper lip of the dog on Mr. Bucklaw's right puckered slightly, exposing two long, curled fangs. Jim heard a growl bubble softly in the dog's throat.

"Easy, Jackson," Bucklaw said.

"Nice dogs," said Jim.

"They don't like strangers."

"No, sir."

"Did that girl ask you to bring her home?"

"No, sir."

"I ain't gonna have a bunch of boys sniffing around after that girl. She ain't in heat. You understand me?"

"Yes, sir."

"This is private property."

"Yes, sir," Jim said. "I know that."

Mr. Bucklaw rapped twice against the roof of the car. "All right, then," he said. "You best get on down the mountain, where you belong."

October 5, 1941

Aliceville, North Carolina
Dear Mr. Dunlap,
 I am writing to you today regarding my son Jim Glass's recent mission of mercy up Lynn's Mountain, about which I am not pleased. He did not return home until well after dark, by which time his uncles and I were beside ourselves with worry. (When he walked in the door, my brothers were preparing to drive up the mountain in search of him, expecting to find God knows what!) Once Jim learned that his Uncle Zeno had already contacted you and learned his whereabouts, he freely admitted that you had not asked him to take Christine Steppe home after she grew ill — as he had at first fibbed to his Uncle Coran — but that he had volunteered for the duty. (You may rest assured that he has since been punished for the lie, as well as for the adventure itself.) You, of course, had no way of knowing that I would have not allowed Jim to take that girl home under any circumstances. (Heaven forbid, what if he had run across her father?) That is why I am writing to inform you that should a like occasion arise in the future, Jim does NOT have my permission, unless you hear differently from me personally, to use his car to provide transportation to needy students, particularly if they live at the ends of the earth. Despite Jim's opinion to the contrary, I do not think that at seventeen years of age he is ready for the medical mission field. In fact, I am no longer convinced that he is even old enough to drive, and only the intercession of

his uncles has prevented me from throwing his car key into the river.
   I am,

Respectfully yours,
Elizabeth McBride Glass

Uncle Zeno and the
White Mule

*J*IM SLEPT late the morning of Big Day, a first for him. Mama twice opened the door of his room and stuck her head in. At the kitchen table Uncle Zeno rattled his newspaper and cleared his throat and set his coffee cup down in its saucer harder than was absolutely necessary. When Jim finally opened his eyes, sometime after eight-thirty, he smiled only slightly at the noise his uncle was making and still didn't get out of bed.

Instead he stared at the ceiling and listened to the lonesome *shush* of cars passing on the highway. It had rained off and on most of the night, and ordinarily the threat of bad weather on Big Day would have worried him. But this year he had no desire to trudge up to the school and walk the same hallways he walked during the week, looking at the fresh Bible story paintings taped to the walls, while the little kids who had painted the pictures ran up and down, shouting to one another, and the teachers who had made the little kids paint the pictures snapped their fingers at them from the doorways as they ran by, and the parents of the little kids, decked out in their good overalls and Sunday dresses, the men with their hats in their hands, tiptoed up and down like they were coming in late to church and studied the pictures and introduced themselves to the teachers. And this year he had no desire to throw rings at hoops or baseballs at milk jugs or darts at balloons or footballs through holes in a wall, not even if girls from New Carpenter or Allendale were watching him do it. Most particularly he had no desire to ride the rides partnered up with Dennis Deane or — even worse — Mama or one of the uncles. This year he didn't want to go to Big Day at all. He had gone to sleep thinking about Bucky Bucklaw and was still thinking about Bucky Bucklaw when he woke up.

Jim had never liked Bucky, not even before Chrissie had moved back. For three years he had played second base while Bucky played shortstop, an injustice if there had ever been one. Bucky had been the kind of baseball player who blamed his glove when he booted a ground ball, or his bat when he struck out. During double-play situations, when he did manage to field a grounder cleanly, he had always run over and stepped on second himself, rather than toss the ball to Jim. And when his throws didn't arrive at first on time (which they never did), more often than not he had glared at Jim and told him to stay out of the way. (Coach Hamrick never said anything to Bucky about blowing all those double plays because he picked apples for Bucklaw Sr. in the fall — everybody knew that.) And now, as if claiming shortstop when he didn't deserve it hadn't been bad enough, Bucky had also claimed Chrissie, against Chrissie's will, and seemed to be getting away with it.

Since their one trip up the mountain the week before, Chrissie had all but stopped speaking to Jim. In history class she stood frowning in the aisle, without really looking at him, until he moved his desk back so that her hair wouldn't land on it. He waited for her every morning at the top of the steps in the vain hope that something had changed, but nothing ever did. He had, for all practical purposes, become invisible to her. Still, he believed that she loved him as much as he loved her — he could tell that by the *way* she didn't look at him — only she couldn't tell him she loved him because she would get in trouble. As a result, Jim carried around a knot in his gut that wouldn't unravel, and his dislike of Bucky had blossomed into a fine hatred. Sometimes he daydreamed about finding Bucky hurting Chrissie somehow and shooting him dead.

When Jim finally made it in to breakfast, he didn't eat much. The eggs tried to climb back out of his throat, the milk smelled sour, and even the biscuits didn't taste good.

"You're losing weight," Mama said. "Are you sick?" She leaned over and tried to put her hand on his forehead, but he moved out of her reach.

"I'm fine," he said. "I'm just getting in shape for base-ball season."

Uncle Zeno folded his newspaper and put it down beside his plate. "You'll never grow hair on your chest if you don't eat more breakfast than that," he said.

"I've already got hair on my chest," said Jim.

"I meant another one."

"Humph."

"I think somebody woke up on the wrong side of the bed this morning," Mama said.

Jim glared at the eggs hardening on his plate.

"Ain't you going to Big Day?" Uncle Zeno asked. "Corrie and Allie are already up there."

"I doubt it," Jim said. "I might go up with Dennis Deane this evening for the dance."

"Come with me this morning and look at the pictures," Mama said.

"They could put the same ones up every year and nobody would notice," Jim said. "They're always the same."

Out of the corner of his eye he saw Mama cast Uncle Zeno a meaningful look.

Uncle Zeno slid his chair noisily away from the table. "Then let's me and you go for a ride."

"Where are we going?" asked Jim.

"To see a man about a dog."

At the stop sign on Depot Street, Jim couldn't help looking up the hill toward the school. Despite the weather, the crowd at Big Day seemed as big as it did every year. Uncle Zeno pulled slowly onto the road, into a creeping line of traffic, and pointed the truck toward New Carpenter. Jim watched the Ferris wheel spinning on the playground, but only a thin memory of the happiness and excitement he used to feel stirred in his chest. He was glad when they finally passed over the railroad tracks and into the countryside, where it wasn't Big Day at all, only Saturday.

Uncle Zeno cleared his throat. "Does Christine Steppe know how bad you're in love with her?"

Jim started, then smiled a little for the second time that morning. "What makes you think I'm in love with Christine Steppe?"

"If you were any more in love with her, we'd have to bury you."

"Being in love never killed anybody."

"You know that ain't right. Being in love is like getting run over. Sometimes it kills you and sometimes it don't."

Jim turned away from Uncle Zeno and stared into the ditch winding by.

"I don't want to talk about it," he said.

"All right, then. We won't talk about it."

"But she's a good girl, Uncle Zeno. I think she's about the best person I ever met."

"I never said she wasn't."

"And I know she loves me, too, but Bucky Bucklaw has told everybody that she's his girlfriend, even though she's not, and since her granddaddy only has one arm and works for Bucky's daddy, she can't go out with me, or Mr. Bucklaw might run the whole bunch of them off, and then what would they do?"

"I don't know."

"And I hate Bucky's guts. He's a terrible baseball player, and I'm sick of him assuming everything in the world belongs to him just because his name is Bucklaw, and I wish he would just, well, die."

"*Jim!*"

"But I *do*. I wish he would die and then I wish his sorry hide would burn in hell."

"You stop it right there," Uncle Zeno said. "That's enough. I don't ever want to hear you say that about anybody. I don't care who it is."

"But it's not fair, what he's doing to her."

"I don't care if it's fair or not. Wishing somebody dead is a terrible thing, a sinful thing, and wishing they would burn in hell is even worse. I want you to be a better man than that."

"But I'm not a better man than that."

"You have to choose to be a good man," Uncle Zeno said. "You have to choose every minute of every day. As soon as you don't, you're lost."

Jim didn't feel like listening to another one of Uncle Zeno's lectures about life, so he tried to head it off. "Fine," he said. "I'll choose to be a good man."

"All right, then."

They rode in silence for a mile or so, but Jim was still angry. "What do y'all have against Chrissie?" he asked.

"I don't know that we have anything against her," Uncle Zeno said. "She might be the best girl to ever come down the mountain. You just need to remember that when you get tangled up with somebody, you get tangled up with their whole family."

"What's wrong with her family? I met her folks. They just seem poor, is all."

"Oh, the McAbees are all right, I guess. Hard times just run 'em down after Nub got his arm cut off. It's Injun Joe that worries me."

"What's wrong with him?"

"He ain't worth killing, that's what."

"Now, how is what I said about Bucky different than what you just said about Chrissie's daddy?"

"I never said I wanted to kill Injun Joe. I just said he wasn't *worth* killing."

"And that's not sinful?"

Uncle Zeno stared resolutely ahead.

"Oh, come on, now," Jim said. "Don't be a hypocrite."

"All right, then, daggummit, Doc, have it your way. It was sinful. I shouldn't have said it. I'll repent for it after while, but that's between me and the Lord. Right now maybe I just want to enjoy it for a minute."

"I think I know why you hate him so much."

"You do, huh?"

"Chrissie told me that you and her mama almost got married."

"Is that right?"

"And I met her mama that day I took Chrissie home. She said to tell you hello."

"Well, wasn't that nice of her."

"And I bet y'all broke up because of Injun Joe."

"And how do you figure this is any of your business?"

Jim shrugged. "If Chrissie can ever figure out how to get out from under the Bucklaws, I'm going to try to marry her, which would make her parents my in-laws."

"You know her daddy's full-blooded, don't you?"

"So?"

"So Chrissie's half Cherokee."

"What difference does that make?"

"I'm just doing the arithmetic. Your babies would be one-quarter Indian. Is that all right with you?"

"It doesn't bother me," Jim said. "They'd still be half Chrissie."

"What if people talked?"

"Since when do we care about people talking? And surely you're not saying that all Indians are bad."

"I don't know nothing about Indians. I don't know if Injun Joe was trouble because he was an Indian, or if he was trouble because he was trouble, but he was already bad news the day he got off the train. I've only ever met one Indian, and he was a bad one. That's all I'm saying."

"That doesn't mean Chrissie's going to turn out bad," Jim said.

"Sometimes the apple don't fall far from the tree."

"And sometimes it does."

"You don't look for apples in a peach orchard, Doc."

"That doesn't make a bit of sense, Uncle Zeno. Is she an apple or a peach? And you never told me if I was right about you and Chrissie's mama."

Uncle Zeno never took his eyes off the road. "If I tell you how it was this once, will you not ask me about it again?"

"Just this once," Jim said. "That'll do."

"The first time I ever laid eyes on Nancy McAbee was at the brush arbor revival in 1916. They built the brush arbor up on the mountain because it was a little cooler than it was down here, and the revival lasted the better part of a week. It was always the second week in July, after everybody had laid their crops by, and people would come from all over. They'd load up in their wagons and head up the mountain and camp out and go to the meetings. They would have four or five preachers there at one time, so when one got wore out with preaching, somebody else could start in. There'd always be a bunch of people get saved or rededicated, and the preachers would take turns baptizing them in the creek, and you heard tell that sometimes when the weather was hot, people got rededicated just because the water was cold.

"That was the year Corrie and Allie and I sang. We had just won the Associational ribbon for the first time, and they asked us to come up and sing at the brush arbor. You should have heard Allie sing back then. He could sing alto pretty as any girl. He can still sing that high, but he won't do it anymore because people made fun of him. Now he'll only sing lead or tenor, as you know, and we don't win the ribbon because there's not enough space between his voice and mine, and you can tell him I said so. Anyway, we had a buckboard then with a hoop top on it, and we had a matched set of white mules named Caesar and Augustus, which you've heard tell about, and me and Mama and Daddy and your uncles and Cissy loaded the wagon and went up for the revival. Me and Corrie and Allie sang every morning and every evening at the start of the service.

"The first or second day of the meeting, I was up there singing, and I looked out in the pews and saw the prettiest little brown-headed girl I'd ever seen. You ever seen a chestnut-colored mare? Well, that's the color Nancy's hair was then. And you wouldn't believe how fair her skin was. So instead of thinking about what I was singing, I was thinking about who that little girl was, and how I could get to know her. This was right after Nub had got his arm cut off at the sawmill. He still looked awful and he was so weak he could hardly get around and they hadn't figured out yet how they were going to live and they came to the brush arbor to pray about it. At one of the services, I remember, we took up a love offering for them.

"One evening after supper, before they started the service, I was watering and brushing Caesar and Augustus down at the creek, and I looked up and saw

Nancy standing on the other bank. All of a sudden she was just there. I didn't even hear her come out of the laurel. When she saw me looking at her she said, 'Where'd you get them white mules?'

"I said, 'At the white mule store. Where'd you get them brown eyes?'

"And she said, 'At the brown eye store.'

"After that I acted like I wasn't going to say anything else. It was always my experience that girls liked you better if you pretended you didn't care anything about them. So I didn't even look at her. When she didn't turn around and go back in the laurel, I knew I was in good shape. After a minute she said, 'One of your brothers sings like a girl.'

"And I said, 'That'd be Allie.'

"She said, 'And he's got a name like a girl, too.'

"I just kept brushing whatever mule it was I was brushing.

"Then she said, 'What's your other brother's name?'

"And I said, 'Corrie.'

"She said, 'And that's a girl's name. Do you have a girl's name, too?'

"I said, 'My name's Colleen. What's yours?' Colleen was my mother's name, of course, but it was the first one I could think of.

"She thought about it a minute and said, 'Bill.'

"And I said, 'Bill, do you want to go walking with me after the service?'

"And she said, 'Colleen, that sounds good.'

"The funny thing about the meeting at the brush arbor was that a whole lot more courting went on up there than you might think. Men who might get their gun and shoot at you if you showed up on a Sunday afternoon in the bright sunshine and asked to speak to their daughter, for some reason up on the mountain would let you go walking with that same daughter after the evening service and it pitch-black dark. I figure it was because back then the roads were bad, and the only people you ever saw were the same bunch who lived in your settlement that you went to school with during the week and church with on Sunday, and most of them were already your cousins, anyway. It was just hard to find somebody to go out with. So, at the brush arbor, while everybody did pay attention to the preaching and the singing and the Holy Spirit came down and people got anointed and baptized, like a regular revival, a lot of boys and girls were looking for somebody they could marry. That's just how it worked. You might not believe it today, but back then boys and girls just couldn't wait for the lay-by time so they could get up to the brush arbor. And when you didn't have a girlfriend, you thought about the brush arbor all year long.

"That first evening, Nancy and I were holding hands before we got out of sight. I still remember how pretty it was. After you got away from the wagons a little bit, you could look back toward the camping ground and see all the campfires burning through the trees and the lanterns hanging up over the wagons, and you could hear the mules stomping around on their pickets and snuffling in their feed bags or cropping on the grass, and you could hear the water running in the creek. If you walked far enough down the trail, you'd come out in the bald, where you could see down in the valley. If you looked hard enough, you might see a lamp or two burning way off in the distance at some farmhouse or other, but mostly it was just dark and still and quiet and up overhead was the moon and the black sky and all the stars."

"Did you kiss her?"

"Of course I kissed her. And after I kissed her, just that one time, I didn't care anything about any of the other little girls I'd been courting down here. I'd liked all of them just fine before Nancy came along, but after I met up with Nancy, they just didn't interest me none. We were going steady before the end of the revival. The only problem, of course, was that she lived up on the mountain, and I lived down here. I had to work six days a week, so Sunday was the only day I could see her. I'd get up before daylight and saddle Caesar and ride up the mountain and get there in time for preaching. Then I'd take dinner with her and her mama and daddy. Of course, I always made sure I had a ham with me, or a chicken, or a peck of potatoes, since I knew they couldn't afford to feed me. Nub had got hurt at Rad Carson's sawmill. They were running a load of ties one day the belt broke and snapped his arm off about six inches above the elbow. Radford felt awful about it, of course, and would've kept Nub on, doing something or other, but Nub felt like that was charity and went on his way. So, I made sure I carried food up there with me when I went to see Nancy. After dinner we would go walking, or sit by the fire if it was cold and pop popcorn or shell walnuts. Then I'd saddle up and ride down the mountain and get home after dark. It wasn't so bad as long as the weather was warm, but when it turned off cold or it was raining, it was a pretty doggone miserable trip. And if you think that road's bad now, you should have seen it then. During the week we wrote letters back and forth."

"When did Injun Joe show up?"

"Hold on, now. Nobody at our house wants to talk about Injun Joe and Nancy McAbee. And I don't want you talking about them to anybody else. You understand?"

"Yes, sir."

"All right, then. Injun Joe. One day, around the time of the brush arbor meeting where I met Nancy, he just got off the train. Nobody around here had ever laid eyes on him before that. He was from somewhere or other up above Cherokee, and he said he'd gone to college down in Raleigh but he'd got in some kind of fight and somebody or other had stole his money. It was quite a tale, and I don't know if there was any truth to it or not. He said he'd started out for home but didn't have the fare to make it all the way back to Dillsboro. He only got as far as Aliceville. If he'd made it to New Carpenter, we never would have heard tell of him. When he got off the train, he didn't have a dime to his name, and Daddy believed what he said and hired him."

"Chrissie's daddy used to work for us?"

"He didn't work for us long. We took him on as a hand, that was the only job we had, but Injun Joe didn't want to be a hand, he wanted to be the boss man. He'd only been here a day or two when he started coming up with ideas about how we could do this or that better than the way we'd been doing it for years."

"What's wrong with that?"

"Well, nothing, I don't guess, initiative's a good thing, but that's not what we were paying him for. We were paying him to work in the field, not tell us how we ought to run our mill or our cotton gin or rotate our crops or what kind of bull we ought to get."

"Were any of his ideas any good?"

"Sure, some of them were. I'll grant him that. Injun Joe was as smart a man as I ever met. He just didn't like his station in life. We noticed right off that he wouldn't have anything to do with the other field hands. He wouldn't even drink water out of the same jar they did. He always lined up to drink water out of our jar. And when dinnertime came, he wanted to come to the house and eat dinner with us. I've never seen anybody hate a black man as much as Injun Joe did."

"Did you let him come to the house?"

"We didn't quite know what to do, to be honest.

None of us had ever met an Indian. When he came to the house, he didn't go around the back, the way the field hands did. He just knocked right on the front door, which surprised us. Then when Cissy or who-ever opened the door, he didn't take his hat off. Mama thought that was awful forward."

"Did he quit?"

"No, we let him go. One day out in the field, we were picking cotton, and he said Abraham's son, Isaac, spit water on his shoe. Isaac's the one that moved to Chicago. I don't think you've ever met him. Now, Isaac might have spit on Joe, he had a temper on him, and maybe it was over the water jar, so I don't know. And it might have been an accident. Isaac said he didn't do it one way or the other. Whatever happened, Joe knocked Isaac down flat on his back and I fired him on the spot."

"Did you fire Isaac?"

"No. Abraham's people have been working here since slave times, and you give people who've worked for you that long the benefit of the doubt. Joe's just lucky I was there and Abraham didn't cut his throat."

"If you fired Injun Joe, how did he wind up mar-ried to Nancy?"

"After I fired Joe, he hated me as much as he hated a field hand. I guess he looked at me and saw every-thing he wanted but didn't have any way of getting, and he saw that I had taken a black man's part over his, in front of other black men. I always figured that he went after Nancy to get me back. But who knows?

Nancy'd been down to visit and had stayed overnight with us, and Joe'd seen her, of course, and maybe seeing her for the first time had the same effect on him that it had on me. I don't know. She was just the prettiest girl. After I fired him, he cleared his stuff out of the storeroom and took off. We figured he was going to walk back to Cherokee, but where he went was straight up the mountain. He worked for Rad Carson a while, but Radford didn't need a foreman any more than we did, he needed somebody to stack lumber, so he caught on with Arthur Bucklaw, working in the fruit trees. Joe said he'd gone down to Raleigh to study forestry, and apparently he had a way with trees and already knew how to graft and prune, and it wasn't long until he was Bucklaw's right-hand man. A lot of those apple and peach trees you see now up on the Bucklaw place Injun Joe planted. The apples have done real well, of course, but more often than not, frost gets the peaches."

"Back up," Jim said. "Did Injun Joe start courting Nancy while she was still your girlfriend?"

"I don't know if you could call it courting, exactly, he was way too smart for that, but he was always just . . . *around*. Nancy'd go down to the store on Saturday, and he'd be there. She'd be walking home from church with some of her girlfriends the Sundays I couldn't make it, and he'd pass them on the road and tip his hat. She'd be sitting on the porch stringing beans with her mama, and he'd just happen to pass by and stop in the edge of the yard and talk for a while.

If he found a bee tree, he'd bring them a comb of honey. It was all real innocent at first, nothing you could call him out on."

"Did you ever get in a fight with him?"

"No, sir. I did not."

"I might've had to fight him, if she'd been my girl-friend."

"I don't believe in fighting a man to keep him away from a woman. Either you can trust a woman or you can't. If you can trust her, nothing anybody can say is going to turn her head, and if you can't trust her, beating up every man who says howdy to her won't do you a bit of good."

"Didn't you worry about him, though?"

"Nah, although, looking back at it now, I obviously should have. As far as I was concerned, he was just some hothead Cherokee buck who didn't have two dimes to rub together. And I trusted Nancy. I never would have thought of Injun Joe as a rival in a million years. What put him over the top on me, though, was the war. The war was going hot and heavy then, and all you heard were people jawing back and forth about whether or not we were going to get in it, or whether or not we should get in it, or whose side we ought to get in it on, and then, in 'seventeen, of course, we got in it, and Wilson started up the draft. I registered, but they never called my number. And I didn't join. I thought about it and prayed about it and studied about it, and I just couldn't figure how I had a dog in that fight. I couldn't see how the king and his bunch and the French and their bunch were any better than the kaiser and his crowd. It seemed to me that everybody had just got bowed up for no good reason and were going to get into it no matter what. I just couldn't see how any of that mess had anything to do with me or mine. I had too much work to do here. So I didn't join.

"Of course boys from New Carpenter and Aliceville and up on the mountain did join, by the trainload, they just lined up to get in. Once we got in the war, you'd read in the papers how the Germans were raping nuns and hanging them from the church steeples, and you'd read how they were marching down the road with babies stuck on their bayonets, but it didn't seem to me like much of it could be true. A lot of people did think it was true, though, and it wasn't long before most of the fighting-age boys around here had either gotten drafted or joined up and gone off to France. When I didn't go, and didn't go, people started to talk. And when boys from here started getting killed, they started getting mad."

"At you?"

"At me. At Nancy. At Corrie and Allie and Mama and Daddy. Your mama. All of us. Homer Ruppe was the first one from here to get killed. He got his foot hung in a ladder on the troopship going over and fell and managed to break his neck before he even got to France. It wasn't but a day or two after his folks got notified that somebody wrung a chicken's neck and threw it up on our porch. It seemed like people just got mean all of a sudden. Most of the time you can live your whole life and the crowd won't even notice you, but once it singles you out, you can't get away from it. People are like a pack of dogs that way. They threw chickens up in the yard, we had a hound or two disappear, they put manure in the mailbox and threw a dead snake in the well, and somebody even painted a bad word on the side of the barn and we had to take off from work and paint over it. And it's all because I didn't join the army."

"You weren't a conscientious objector, were you?"

"No, sir. I was not. I was somebody who didn't get drafted. And not joining the service when I wasn't drafted was my Constitutional right. Injun Joe saw which way the wind was blowing, though, and he started to run me down bigger than any of them. Never to my face, I guess I would've had to fight him over that, but you'd hear tell down here how he was up on the mountain, flapping his jaws. Sometime along the way, he started running me down to Nancy, telling her how I was a coward, how I didn't care about my country, how I was going to let the kaiser march up the mountain and rape all the girls before I decided to do anything. I still rode up the mountain on Sundays to see Nancy, but I noticed that people up there stopped speaking to me after church and saying howdy when I passed them on the road, and I'd see them whispering when I went by. And it was hard on Nancy, I know it was. If I was the coward, then she was the coward's girl. She started asking me, wasn't I going to join the army, wasn't I going to join the army, was I afraid of the Germans, and this or that, and it finally got to be a hard place between us. We'd gotten engaged Christmas in nineteen seventeen, and the next March she broke up with me. Injun Joe joined up sometime in there, and with me out of the way he somehow talked Nancy into marrying him before he shipped out. One Sunday afternoon, they just walked down to the preacher's house. To this day I don't know how in the world he managed it.

"Then things just went from bad to worse. Coran and Al got tired of people running us down and throwing dead chickens in the yard, and as soon as they turned eighteen, they run off and joined the army without telling anybody they were going."

"I never knew Uncle Coran and Uncle Al were in the army."

"They weren't in it long. The war ended, thank the Lord, before they finished their training, but before they could get mustered out, most of the boys in their camp came down with the flu and they got quarantined. When they finally got out of quarantine, they started on home, but the flu beat them here. As you know, that's how Mama and Daddy died. The flu killed fourteen people in Aliceville that year. Later on, everybody said that Coran and Al were the ones who brought it here, but that was a bald-faced lie. Mama and Daddy were already on their deathbeds before their train even got here, and it's all wrote down in the Bible if anybody wants to see it. Of course, after all the funerals and the flu talk, Coran and Al couldn't even get a girl to look at them. Between that and me not going to the war and Mama and Daddy dying and us trying to figure out how to run things on our own, I guess that's how we all got set in our ways and ended up bachelors."

"Y'all could still get married," Jim said.

"Oh, it's nice to think so, I guess, but I figure that ship sailed off to France or somewhere a long time ago. Nancy McAbee was the only girl I ever came close to marrying."

"What did Chrissie mean when she told me she didn't know where her daddy was?"

"If I tell you, you have to promise you won't mention it to a soul."

"I promise."

"Because if this got out, it would bring hardship down on Nancy and that girl, and they don't need any more of that."

"I swear I won't tell anybody. What did he do?"

"He robbed a bank, and he shot a policeman. The law can't find him. That's why Nancy and Chrissie came home."

In New Carpenter, Jim sat in Uncle Zeno's truck and stared at the window of the hardware store. Most of what he could see in the glass was the reflection of the world behind him: the line of farm trucks sniffing out parking places; people scurrying between the awnings of the stores across the street as though it were still raining; the lettering on the store windows backward and foreign-looking. All he could see inside the hardware store were a display of canning jars and the occasional passing shadow of a clerk or customer. Uncle Zeno was in there somewhere, but Jim didn't know where. He had elected to wait in the truck rather than going in to gawk at the fishing plugs and the pocketknives and the dark, glamorous pistols. He thought he was getting a little old for that.

It seemed as though there were good reasons to be mad at all of the people in Uncle Zeno's story and — save Injun Joe and the people who ran down Jim's family — an equal number of good reasons not to be. He was disappointed in Uncle Zeno for not joining the army but simultaneously proud of him for continuing to ride that white mule up the mountain, even though the world had turned against him. It was easy for him to work up a satisfying case of contempt for Chrissie's mother but equally easy to feel sorry for her when he considered how hard her life had turned out. She had obviously picked the wrong man. And while her choosing Injun Joe had somehow locked Uncle Zeno into a permanent bachelorhood, it had also eventually led to Jim watching Chrissie walk around the front of the bus on the first day of school. If Uncle Zeno had married Nancy, Chrissie — if she had been born at all — would have been his cousin. He didn't know what to think about her lying to him about Injun Joe. He knew that if word got out, she would probably be hounded out of school, but he also wondered, now that she had proved she was capable of it, if she was lying to him about anything else. Maybe she really did love Bucky; maybe she just wanted to string Jim along for fun, or as a spare. No matter how Jim tried to follow the story in his mind, it never led to a satisfactory destination, only to a new place to begin thinking about it. Eventually the door of the store swung open and Uncle Zeno appeared with a logging chain looped over one shoulder. He threw the chain heavily into the bed of the truck before climbing into the cab.

"What's wrong with the chain you got back at the house?" Jim asked.

"Nothing, I don't guess. I just thought it might be handy to have a longer one."

"Do you still love her?"

Uncle Zeno reached for the starter, but paused. "Nah," he eventually said. "Let's go home."

Back in Aliceville, Uncle Zeno parked the truck in the yard. Jim got out and walked backward toward the porch. The sky had cleared slightly, and on top of the hill the rides spun in a thin sunlight that neither looked nor felt quite warm. A breeze had freshened in the north, and on it rode the manufactured screams of people pretending to be scared, the crazed hooting of the calliope, and the good carnival smells of sawdust and popcorn and engine exhaust and burned sugar. Jim closed his eyes and inhaled deeply, but just once, then turned his back on Big Day and strode into the house. Mama's door was closed. Uncle Zeno tiptoed down the hallway and out the back door. Jim thought about going squirrel hunting, but the woods seemed too far away and he dreaded the prospect of cleaning whatever he shot. He retreated into his room and lay down on the bed and tried reading the Zane Grey novel that had come in the mail that week, but he put the book down as soon as the penniless cowboy protagonist fell in love with the raven-haired daughter of the ranch owner. That happened in all the books. He crossed his hands on his chest and decided to think about baseball. When he opened his eyes it was dusk outside and the uncles were talking around the kitchen table and Mama was calling him to supper.

Dance Lessons

JIM WALKED up the hill toward the school with Dennis Deane. The breeze that had come up during the afternoon had blown the clouds off to the south before falling quiet at sunset, leaving the air chilled but pleasant, the stars close overhead. Up ahead the school building was dark, except for the tall gymnasium windows which threw light across the broad, sloping backs of the cars parked in the schoolyard. In the distance Jim could hear the furious sawing of a fiddle, the *doom-Doom, doom-Doom, doom-Doom* of a bass, and the rumbling *choonk-Choonk choonka-choonk, choonk-Choonk choonka-choonk* of clogging square dancers. The band was a good one — Joe Doug Revis and the Cherry Bounce Boys, all the way from Whittier — but Jim had already decided that he wasn't going to dance with anybody, no matter what. Not pretty, rich girls from New Carpenter, nor wild mill-hill girls from the towns on the other side of the river, not even if they grabbed his hand and pleaded and tried to drag him onto the floor. The only reason he was going was so that everybody could see how miserable he was. And if nobody told Chrissie how miserable he was, the evening would be a waste of time.

Maybe, he thought, he should just forget about the dance altogether and go coon hunting. It wasn't too cold, the woods would be wet from the rain earlier in the day, and the dogs would be able to trail easily. He would have a hard time, however, dragging the uncles out of the gym and getting them to go with him. They didn't dance much, but they loved listening to a string band. And they hardly ever went coon hunting on Saturday night. They said it made them too sleepy during church the next day.

What Jim really wished was that he was going to the dance with Chrissie. They would dance for a while — only with each other — and when Mama and the uncles went home, he would drive her through the fields down to the river. On the way she would scoot up close beside him and he would hold her hand — except when he had to change gears. (Maybe, though, he could put his arm around her and work the clutch and she could change the gears.) At the river they would cuddle up in the rumble seat beneath a blanket and listen to the water and look at the stars. Chrissie's nose would be cold and he would feel it on his cheek when he kissed her.

Of course, Jim had never actually cuddled up with

a girl in the rumble seat of the Major, and his pros-
pects didn't seem to be getting any better. Norma
had steadfastly refused, and there was fat chance of
getting Chrissie anywhere near his car. If he welded
the rumble seat shut it wouldn't make any difference.
He might as well sell the daggum car for all the good
it was doing him. He looked over at Dennis Deane
and disgustedly jammed his hands into the pockets
of his jacket. Going to square dances with Dennis
Deane was not how he had imagined spending his
senior year.

"Tell me something," Dennis Deane said. "Why are
we walking up this hill when you have a car?"

"Because the school is only three hundred yards
from my house."

"But, Jim, it's a *steep* hill."

"Stop whining, Dennis Deane. I'm taking you home
after the dance. Isn't that good enough for you?"

"Does that mean we're going steady?"

"Not hardly."

"Well, then I just might catch a ride home with
somebody else."

"Who?"

"I don't know yet. I've cooked up a new secret saying to make girls fall in love with me, and I'm turning
it loose tonight."

Jim waited.

"You wanna hear it?" asked Dennis Deane.

"Nope."

"Oh, come on."

"If I let you tell me, will you shut up?"

"I promise I'll never speak to you again as long as I live."

"Then you've got a deal," Jim said.

"Okay. You be the girl."

"I don't want to be the girl."

"Well, you can't be me, because you don't know the secret saying."

"I don't want to be you, either."

"Everybody wants to be me."

"No, they don't."

"Damn it, Jim, will you shut up for just one minute and listen to my secret saying? I need to practice it before the shooting starts."

Jim huffed but didn't say anything.

"That's better," Dennis Deane said. "You're a girl."

"I'm a girl."

"I walk up to you and I say, 'Hey there, Red Riding Hood, I'm the big, bad wolf.'"

Jim stopped in the road and stared at Dennis Deane. "That's it?"

"Of course not. Then I say, 'Do you want to see my long, bushy tail?'"

Jim shook his head and started again up the hill. "That's about the stupidest thing I ever heard," he said.

"Then how about, 'I'll huff and I'll puff and I'll pull your drawers down'?"

"That's even worse. Now you've got stuff from two different stories. It's not even the same wolf."

"Well, if you're so smart, let's hear your secret saying to make girls fall in love with you."

"Have a nice trip," Jim said.

"I don't get it."

"That's because there's nothing to get. If I had a secret saying to make girls fall in love with me, I wouldn't be walking up this daggum hill with you, now, would I?"

Dennis Deane was quiet for a few steps. "You just need to forget about Pocahontas," he said.

"I've asked you to not call her names," said Jim.

"She's Bucky Bucklaw's girlfriend, for God's sake. Don't you even wonder what kind of girl would go out with an idiot like that in the first place?"

"You don't know anything about it."

"And you keep saying that. Meantime, there's a whole gym full of *available* girls right up there, Jim, just raring to go. All you have to do is pick one out."

"Just raring to go, are they, Dennis Deane?"

"You know they are. Nothing makes a girl go crazy like square dancing. That's a scientific fact."

"I must've slept through that class."

"But it's *true*," Dennis Deane said. "All that clogging gets everything bouncing up and down and makes it all loosey-goosey and lovey-dovey."

"You belong in Broughton with the rest of the nuts."

"Just try it out, if you don't believe me. Ask somebody to dance. I dare you. You can even use my secret saying."

"Thanks, but no thanks."

When they reached the schoolyard, Jim threaded his way through the haphazardly parked cars and trucks with Dennis Deane close on his heels. The gymnasium windows were so brightly lit that the glare made it difficult for him to see where he was going.

"I can't see too good," Dennis Deane said.

"That ain't exactly news."

"What if we run up on Injun Joe out here in the dark?"

"We ain't gonna run up on Injun Joe."

"How do you know? I heard he might be anywhere."

"You don't know what you're talking about."

"Injun Joe?" Dennis Deane whispered. "Hello? Chief? You out here?"

"Cut it out," Jim said. "You're not funny."

He spotted a small group of grown men smoking up ahead and circled around to avoid them. Anybody hanging around the schoolyard during the dance was probably drinking, and anybody drinking would sooner or later be looking for a fight.

"You ought to be more worried about lintheads, anyway."

"I ain't worried about nobody," said Dennis Deane. "Lintheads. Injuns. Tall girls. Bring 'em on."

When they finally reached the front steps, it felt

like home base in some not particularly fun playground game against much older boys. From the
landing he turned and looked back across the schoolyard. With the light now at his back, it didn't look
scary at all.

Dennis Deane suddenly punched him on the arm.

"Ow. What was that for?"

"Daggummit, Jim. This is our last Big Day before
we graduate."

"So?"

"So just forget about her. Have some fun for once
in your life."

"Go show somebody your bushy tail."

"Oh, I'm planning on it."

Inside the gymnasium, the floor was ringed with a
crowd seven or eight people deep. The air was hot
and close, stale with cigarette smoke, even though the
tall windows were raised. The music — a reel Jim
didn't recognize — thumped and twanged over top
of the thunderous stomping of the dancers. Jim could
feel the floor spring beneath his feet in perfect time
to the song and wondered what kept it from falling in.
When he worked his way to the edge of the floor, he
found squares of dancers cutting needle-and-thread
figures on what seemed like every available inch of
open space. When the sharply amplified voice of the
caller sang out, "All join hands," the squares unraveled and formed into two large circles, one inside the
other. The circles slowly began to spin in opposite directions, a sight that never failed to impress Jim, no

matter what kind of mood he was in. When the circles got up to speed, they generated a breeze that felt cool on his face. The breeze carried the scents of denim and gingham and calico and hair oil and tobacco and sweat and perfume and hot breath all rolled into a single warm smell that seemed somehow manufactured by the music. Jim turned around to ask Dennis Deane if he could feel the breeze, but Dennis Deane had disappeared.

At the far end of the gym floor, the Cherry Bounce Boys frailed at their instruments on the small stage, beneath a printed banner bearing their name and an advertisement for flour. They wore white shirts and red string ties and matching white cowboy hats, except for Joe Doug himself, whose black hat, cocked just so, identified him as the leader. Romeo Paris was the caller. In front of the band he gripped the microphone with both hands and rocked back and forth and smiled broadly at the spinning circles he had conjured. He was a preacher from New Carpenter who called cattle auctions and square dances on the side. The uncles explained away his name and slightly scandalous avocations by pointing out that he was a Presbyterian. Jim tapped his foot along with the music but stopped as soon as he noticed. He didn't want anyone to think he was having a good time.

The Cherry Bounce Boys played the chorus through one more time and, on a signal from Joe Doug, ended the song on a shave-and-a-haircut, two-bits. The circles slowed and stopped and began to dissolve almost instantly, like smoke rings. Romeo Paris announced that the band was taking a break. The dancers, some of them still clapping, drifted past Jim toward the refreshment table and the door, their voices a happy buzz whose component parts were indistinguishable. Over there, Mama was leaving the floor holding on to Uncle Coran's elbow with both hands, laughing as he told her a joke. Mama loved to square-dance as much as anybody Jim knew but would do so only with him or her brothers. Over here, Norma was thanking Buster Burnette for the dance and trying politely to back away. Jim smiled bitterly. Buster had bad acne and was dumb as a rock and had no idea he was a charity case. Jim would try to remember to sic Dennis Deane on him Monday morning.

He was looking around for Ellie Something, to make sure she knew how unhappy he was so she could tell Chrissie, when he saw Chrissie walking toward him, escorted by an older guy he had never seen before. The guy was tall, with dark, slicked-back hair. He wore sharply pressed suit pants and a shirt and necktie and two-tone gangster shoes. His necktie had flowers painted on it. Jim felt instantly ashamed of the dungarees and high-tops and letter jacket he was wearing, the uniform he wore every single day of his life, which identified him as nothing more than a boy.

When the stranger put his hand in the middle of Chrissie's back to steer her through the crowd, Jim felt a sudden, sharp pain like a punch in his stomach. The guy was obviously Chrissie's *date*, not someone who had simply asked her to dance. She had ridden all the way down here in his *car* — a Pontiac, at least, judging from the looks of the guy, maybe even a Buick — and after the dance they would drive together all the way back up the mountain. Somewhere along the way, the guy would pull off the road into some dark spot and cut the headlights; Chrissie would turn to him and smile. Jim's soul flooded with hatred, not just for the stranger but for Chrissie. She had obviously lied to him about her predicament with Bucky Bucklaw just to get him off her back, and now this stranger was going to put his arms around her and kiss her, when Jim could not.

When Chrissie saw Jim she stopped for a moment and stared. Jim saw her eyes widen. He had caught her. He stared back at her with angry satisfaction, slowly shaking his head in disapproval. She turned and stood on her tiptoes and whispered something into the guy's ear, then turned and started quickly for the door near the bandstand on the far side of the gym. Before the guy followed Chrissie, he stared blankly in Jim's direction but obviously didn't know who or what he was looking for. "You're looking for me, chief," Jim said, but the crowd was too noisy, the stranger too far away, to hear him.

Jim watched them cross the floor and leave the gym together, then forced his way through the crowd and into the hallway. He heard Mama call after him, but he didn't stop. He thought he was going to be sick, and he knew that the restroom would be crowded. He banged open the door to the stairway and ran up the steps into the darkened hallway on the second floor. He ran past Miss Brown's room and kicked open the door of the bathroom, where he startled two young boys, maybe ten years old, who were leaning against the sinks importantly smoking cigarettes.

"Get out of here," Jim said.

"You ain't my daddy," the larger of the two boys said.

Jim felt himself shaking. He stepped forward and slapped the cigarette out of the kid's mouth.

"Get out of here now!" he yelled.

The boys clawed at the door in a panic as they tried to get away. Jim listened to them running down the hallway. He went into a stall and sat down on the toilet and shoved the heels of his hands into his eyes but could not stop seeing Chrissie turn toward the stranger inside the stranger's darkened car. The stranger stroked her hair. Jim got on his knees in front of the toilet and waited to throw up, but nothing happened. He couldn't get sick and he couldn't get better. He thought about praying but didn't want to humble himself, to anybody, when he hadn't done anything wrong. He was the one who had been lied to. Eventually he became aware of the dull percussion of the stomping dancers working its way through the floor. He got up and washed his face. From the mirror over the sink some stupid boy in a stupid jacket stared back at him. He trudged back downstairs and into the gym, even though it was the last place on earth he wanted to be. Sure enough, as soon as he shoved his way through the crowd, he spotted Chrissie happily dancing with her date. She laughed as she ducked and twirled beneath the guy's arm.

Jim spent the rest of the evening watching her. He watched her while she danced, the way her hair bounced and jumped from side to side on her back as she clogged, marking time to the music, a sight that twisted his heart like a rag. He watched her while she drank punch and talked with the stranger on the sidelines during the few songs they sat out. She glanced at him only occasionally, never long enough to see in his eyes how much he despised her. The stranger never looked at him at all. The Cherry Bounce Boys played what seemed like ten thousand songs. Romeo Paris called dance after dance after dance. He knew all the dances in the world. When Jim pushed up his sleeve and looked at his watch, he was surprised to see that it was only ten minutes until ten, and not the darkest middle of the longest night of his life.

Ellie Something tugged on his sleeve.

He leaned toward her so that she could hear him over the music. "Go away," he said.

"I need to talk to you."

"I don't want to hear it, whatever it is."

"I've got a message from Chrissie."

Ellie Something's cheeks and lips were flushed, and she stared at him intently. He raised his eyebrows and waited.

"Chrissie says, cut it out."

"Cut what out?"

"You know what."

"Tell Chrissie she can kiss my long, bushy tail."

Ellie Something looked startled. "What did you just say?" she asked.

"You heard me," Jim said. "Now, go away."

"No," she said firmly. "Chrissie's my friend and you're going to get her in trouble."

"How can I possibly get somebody like that in trouble? She's already a liar and a tramp."

"I'm not going to tell her you said that."

"I don't care what you tell her."

Ellie Something stomped her foot.

"I ought to just slap you silly," she said. "That boy she's with is Bucky's cousin, from over by Casar. The only way the Bucklaws would let her come down here to a dance was if that boy right there brought her. This is her senior year, too, you know, and this is her Big Day as much as it is your Big Day, and you stand over here like some kind of hotshot, staring at people like you know everything, when you don't know nothing about anything."

"Wait a minute," Jim said. "That's Bucky's *cousin?*"

"From over by Casar. He brought her all the way down

here as a *favor*. All Chrissie wanted to do was come to a dance before she graduated. Just one. Her daddy never would let her go to a dance in Oklahoma, and now she's got the Bucklaws to worry about. So the last thing she needs is you treating her like she's trash."

Jim stared darkly at the stranger. "I'm sick of the Bucklaws," he said. "I'm sick of them thinking they own everybody and I'm sick of them pushing people around."

"She's not crazy about them, either, you know."

"What kind of car does he drive?"

Ellie Something's eyes widened comically. She grabbed his sleeve and twisted it.

"*No!*" she cried. "Promise me you won't do anything! You'll get her in so much trouble. The Bucklaws might make her quit school and stay in that awful cabin, and then she won't be able to go anywhere ever again in her whole life. *Promise* me, if you love her as much as you act like you do, you won't do anything at all."

"Let go," Jim said.

"Promise me."

"All right, already. I promise."

Ellie Something patted the wrinkles on his sleeve. "Okay," she said. "Good."

"I just wanted to know what kind of car the jerk drove. That's all."

"Oh. Sorry. I thought you wanted to fight him. It's a black one, I think."

"It ain't him I want to fight," Jim said. "Will you give her a message for me?"

"I don't know. It depends on what it is."

"Tell her I said . . ."

"That you love her?" She batted her eyes at him and giggled.

Jim blushed. "Oh, Lord, Ellie, *no.* Just tell her I said that . . . she looks nice when she dances."

"For such a stuck-up boy, you sure can come up with some sweet things to say."

"Cut it out," he said.

Norma and Dennis Deane appeared on his other side. "Jim," Norma interrupted, "we need to talk."

On the dance floor, Chrissie was waltzing gracefully with Bucky's cousin. Jim had never learned how to waltz, even though Mama had offered to teach him. He wondered who had taught Chrissie.

"I'm tired of talking," he said.

"You're gonna want to hear this," Dennis Deane said. "Hey, there, Ellie Something."

Ellie Something's face instantly went red. "Hey, there, Dennis Deane."

"Jim, this is *very, very, very* important," said Norma. She leaned around Jim and spoke to Ellie Something. "If you'll excuse us, please."

Ellie Something placed her hand on Jim's arm. "Don't worry, *Jim,*" she said. "I'll give you-know-who your message." Then she crinkled her nose at Norma and stalked off.

"What was that all about?" Norma asked. "Who's that nosy little girl delivering your messages to?"

"Nobody," Jim said.

"What were you two talking about, anyway?" asked Dennis Deane.

"*Nothing,*" Jim said. "I thought y'all said you had something important to tell me."

"We do," said Norma. She tilted her head toward the gym entrance. "Don't stare, but look over there and tell me what you see."

Jim moved his head slightly and looked toward the door. The kid whose cigarette he had slapped onto the floor was pointing in his direction. Gathered around him were eight or ten tough-looking guys in their twenties. Mill hands. They were all staring his way. The kid was talking a mile a minute.

"Uh-oh," Jim said.

"Please tell me you didn't slap that little boy," said Norma.

"I didn't exactly *slap* him," Jim said. "But I can see why he might be telling people that."

"I don't know what you did to him, but the little bastard's telling every linthead he can find that you slapped him in the face," Dennis Deane said. "Norma heard him out in the hall and came and got me."

Jim looked around wildly. "Are the uncles still here?"

"No," Norma said. "They left about an hour ago."

"So that makes you General Custer," Dennis Deane said.

"We've got to get you out of here," said Norma.

"How?"

"Door by the stage," Dennis Deane said. "Before they get organized and head us off at the pass."

"Dance with me," said Norma.

"Now?" Jim said. "Are you crazy?"

"No, silly. Waltz me over to that door."

"But I don't know *how* to waltz."

"You daggum better learn," said Dennis Deane.

Norma held out her arms. "Remember. It just goes one-two-three, one-two-three."

Jim sought out Chrissie and Bucky's cousin and watched them and silently counted. Then he looked over at the gym door. The kid was still talking and pointing. Jim had never seen so many lintheads in his life. Wasn't anybody working second shift?

"One-two-three, one-two-three," he said out loud.

"All right, all right," Dennis Deane said. "Everybody knows how to count. Now just count your way over to that damn door and run like hell."

Jim took Norma's right hand in his left and placed his right hand in the middle of her back. Norma smiled and blushed a little. She looked very pretty. What had he been thinking when he broke up with her? She wasn't *that* bad. He looked down at his feet, which looked huge and so far showed no inclination to start dancing.

"One-two-three," Norma said.

Jim rocked back and forth without quite going any-where.

Norma giggled. "Stop moving your lips," she said. "I'm counting."

"Count faster," said Dennis Deane. "Maybe skip some numbers."

"Move me out onto the floor," said Norma. "No. Left foot first. Good. Here we go. Here we go. One-two-three. One-two-three. Don't go straight toward the door, or they'll know what you're doing. But don't get us too close to them, either. They might grab you. And stop stepping on my feet."

He looked down. His feet didn't seem so much to be dancing as they did violently pursuing Norma's. "Sorry," he said.

"Stop looking at your feet," she said.

"I'm not. I'm looking at your feet."

"Well, stop it. You've got to watch where you're going."

"Norma, stop leading."

"I'm not leading," she said. "I'm just trying to keep you from running over somebody."

Jim turned Norma so that she was facing the door. "Are they coming?"

"No. But they're still talking to that little boy. Keep going."

He tried turning Norma again so that he could look for himself, but ran solidly into someone behind him. When he turned he found himself face-to-face with Bucky's cousin.

"Careful, there, friend," the guy said.

"Sorry," said Jim.

Chrissie looked furious. She stared angrily at Jim and mouthed the words, *Leave. Me. Alone.*

"Excuse me?" Norma said.

"Sorry," Jim said again, his face burning. "I'm sorry. Well, bye." He gave up trying to waltz and began pushing Norma more or less directly toward the door.

Norma tried to look back over her shoulder. "Slow down, Jim," she said. "Slow down. You've got to make it look good."

"I don't care how it looks," he said.

As they passed the bandstand, Joe Doug looked down at them and winked and touched his hat with his forefinger. Norma stepped away from Jim but held on to his left hand. She pushed open the door. On the landing outside, Romeo Paris was smoking a cigarette, which he hurriedly tried to hide in his palm when he saw them.

"Excuse us, Reverend," Norma said, starting down the steps.

"Where are you two running off to in such a hurry in the dark?" he asked.

"To see a man about a dog," Jim said.

"Pray for us," Norma called over her shoulder.

At the bottom of the stairs, still holding Norma's hand, Jim broke into a run. They sprinted around the corner of the building and into the schoolyard, where they crouched and ducked between the parked cars. With the light from the gym behind him, he had no trouble seeing and was able to pick a path through the maze at almost full speed. When they cleared the cars, they sprinted down the driveway toward town. They had a good head start, but Norma wasn't very fast. He couldn't tell over the sound of her shoes scuffing the pavement if anybody was chasing them. Below them, all three of the uncles' houses were dark. Everybody had already gone to bed. *Wake up*, Jim thought. *Wake up!* When they reached the bottom of the hill they crossed the highway without breaking stride. The road felt like the boundary of enemy territory, so he slowed and looked back over his shoulder. He didn't immediately see anyone, so he stopped altogether for a better look. He heard Norma panting beside him. He felt a pulse pounding in his palm but couldn't tell if it was hers or his. Nobody was chasing them. Jim felt strangely disappointed. A minute ago, he had been important enough for a posse of lintheads to want to kill him. Now he wasn't important at all. He should have stayed and fought, even if it meant getting beaten up.

"It worked," Norma said.

"Stupid lintheads," Jim said.

"That's an ugly word, Jim."

"Don't start on me, Norma."

"I'm just saying they can't help where they work."

"Yeah, but they can help being stupid," he said. He turned away from the school, dragging Norma behind him.

At Depot Street, they turned automatically toward Uncle Coran's store. When they were dating, he had walked her home from his house by cutting between the store and the building where Uncle Coran kept fertilizer and feed. Norma lived on Raleigh Street, on the other side of the cotton gin. As they passed the shed where Jim parked the Major, he stopped and pulled Norma toward him and wrapped his arms around her and kissed her. When she started to say something, he kissed her again. To his surprise, she began kissing him back. She put her hand on the back of his neck. He had forgotten how good the lilac soap she used smelled on her skin and how soft her lips were. She was a good kisser when you could get her to do it.

He pulled her into the shed and opened the rumble seat of the Major. He helped her over the fender and into the back of the car. He climbed in after her and began kissing her again. Every time he started to think about running away from the lintheads, every time he remembered the look on Chrissie's face as she told him to leave her alone, he kissed Norma harder. And every time he kissed her harder, she kissed him back. When he reached inside her sweater and rubbed the front of her blouse, she did not stop him. Back when they were dating, she would have slapped his knuckles raw for even trying that. That she would let him put his hand inside her sweater now, when she knew he loved Chrissie, suddenly made him sad. Whatever he had been trying to hold up by kissing Norma collapsed on top of him. He stopped kissing her and leaned back and stared straight up into the blackest blackness he had ever seen. He knew it was only the underside of the shed roof, but he imagined it was the sky, without form and void, the stars burned out for good. When he turned to look at Norma, he could see that she was looking at him, but he couldn't make out her expression, only the whiteness of her skin, and the two deep holes where her eyes should have been.

"Norma," he said. "I . . ."

"Shh," she said, placing her fingers on his lips. "Don't."

"But . . ."

"Please don't apologize to me, Jim. That would be the worst thing you could say to me right now. I know you don't love me."

"Then why . . . ?"

She shrugged. "Because I still love you, I guess."

Jim miserably shook his head. "Oh, Norma," he said. "You shouldn't love me."

"You don't get to decide that, Jim. If I want to love you, I can. It's really, well, none of your business who I love."

"Why don't you just find another boyfriend?"

"Because I'm going to college in the fall. I'm going to be a math teacher, Jim, and I'm going to marry somebody who doesn't live in this little-bitty town. I'm going to learn advanced algebra and geometry and I hope trigonometry and calculus. And I'm going to live in a big town, like Charlotte, or Greensboro. But not here, Jim. Not in Aliceville."

"But you were going to marry me."

"You're not going to stay here any more than I am."

"I guess so," Jim said. "But right now I can't think of anyplace in the world I want to be. Here included."

"You don't have to think about that now." She picked up his hand in both of hers. She inhaled through her nose and sighed deeply. "I know it doesn't mean anything to you, but right now I wish you would kiss me some more."

"I don't understand you," he said. "You always said no when we were dating."

"Well, I'm going to tell you a secret, Jim, just this once. Saying no is the only power a girl has in this world. A girl who doesn't say no doesn't have anything at all."

Jim nodded. Chrissie said only no to him, and she had all the power in the world; Norma saying yes just made him feel sorry for her. He helped her down out of the Major and walked her over to Raleigh Street. They didn't talk on the way. Norma walked with her arms crossed but she refused Jim's letter jacket. On her front porch they hugged awkwardly, patting each other's back, just as the porch light blinked on.

"Well," Jim said, "some things never change."

Norma turned toward the door. "And some things do," she said.

BOOK III

Unexpected News

Target Practice

DENNIS DEANE was acting strange, or at least stranger than usual. First, he missed an entire week of school, although the uncles reported seeing him riding his bicycle all over town. But whenever they asked him if he needed a lift somewhere, or why he wasn't in school, or, finally, on Friday, why he had been riding his bicycle around in circles all week, he pretended not to hear them. He just kept pedaling. Then, when Jim drove to Dennis Deane's house Sunday afternoon to pick him up, he found Dennis Deane crouched in the scraggly troop of malnourished cedar trees across the driveway from the Deanes' mailbox. Jim stopped and rolled down the window.

"What are you doing in there?" he asked.

"This used to be my secret hiding place," Dennis Deane said.

"I know. So, what are you doing in there now?"

"Hiding."

"You know I can see you, don't you?"

"Yeah, I guess so."

"So, who are you hiding from?"

"I can't tell you."

"Why not?"

"Are you alone?" Dennis Deane asked.

"What?"

"I said, are you alone?"

"Am I alone," Jim said slowly.

"Did anybody follow you out here?"

Jim frowned at Dennis Deane.

"Damn it, Jim, I ain't fooling around," Dennis Deane said. "I'm trying to keep a lookout here. Did you notice anybody following you?"

"The Lone Ranger," Jim said. "The Lone Ranger followed me. I think I lost Tonto, though."

Dennis Deane paused, apparently weighing his chances against the Lone Ranger riding alone versus his chances against the Lone Ranger and Tonto together. Finally he hurried out of the trees and into Jim's car. His hair was greasy and he didn't smell particularly good. He slammed the door, slid down in the seat, and put his feet up on the dashboard.

"Go," he said.

"Take your feet down."

"What?"

"I'm not driving anywhere until you get your dirty feet off my dashboard."

"There. You happy now?"

"You wanna ride over to New Carpenter?"

"I don't care!" Dennis Deane almost shouted. "Just stop jawing at me and go somewhere!"

Jim popped the clutch, steered the Major sideways, and spun a roostertail of mud all over the mailbox.

"What in the world's wrong with you?" Jim said. "You're acting like some kind of idiot."

Much to Jim's surprise, Dennis Deane jammed the heels of his hands into his eyes and fell over onto the seat. His head lay almost in Jim's lap; Jim shifted uncomfortably toward the door.

"Ohhh," Dennis Deane moaned. "I *am* an idiot. And I'm dead. I'm a big dead idiot."

"What's the matter?"

"Deader'n a doornail, Jim. Deader'n hell. Deader'n dead people."

"Why are you dead?"

"Because they're going to kill me."

"Who's going to kill you?"

"The hillbillies."

"What hillbillies?"

"All of 'em, Jim," Dennis Deane said. "All the hillbillies. They're probably coming down the mountain right now." He sat up straight and looked behind the car so earnestly that Jim glanced in the mirror to see if anyone was following them.

"Why are the hillbillies coming down the mountain?"

"Hey, that sounds like a joke."

"Dennis Deane . . ."

"They'll be riding six white horses when they come, the hillbilly bastards. You just wait."

"What did you do, Dennis Deane?"

"I can't tell you. Can we go to the river? We go to New Carpenter every Sunday. I hate New Carpenter. All the people are tall. Did you ever notice that? Even the girls. All tall." He lay down in the seat again and covered his eyes with his forearm. "Oh, God, I'm dead," he said.

"We can go to the river if you'll tell me why the hillbillies are going to kill you."

"Can I shoot your .twenty-two?"

"If you'll tell me."

Dennis Deane looked up at Jim with one eye from behind his arm. "How many shots?" he asked. He loved to shoot Jim's rifle, but he never bought shells. He didn't have a rifle of his own.

"Six," Jim said.

"Fourteen," replied Dennis Deane.

"Fourteen? You're crazy. Eight."

"Twelve."

"Ten," said Jim. "And that's all."

Dennis Deane shook his head. "You always were stingy," he said. "But all right."

Jim turned the Major around and drove back through Aliceville. Nobody seemed to be roaming the streets looking for Dennis Deane, which Jim duly reported. East of town, he turned off the highway and followed the two muddy tracks of the farm road through the uncles' walnut grove, across the branch, and around the edge of the corn bottom. The field was empty now, save for the shocks of fodder; the uncles and the field hands had pulled the ears earlier in the fall. Brown weeds scraped against the undercarriage of the car. On the far side of the bottom, Jim parked the Major and got his rifle and a box of shells from behind the seat. Dennis Deane sat up and blinked and looked around cautiously. He got out of the car and followed Jim along the narrow path through the woods toward the green smell of the river; they couldn't hear it at first because of the noise they made walking through the leaves. The day was cool, but the sun shone on the large flat rock by the water. The river wandered in from the west but at the rock turned decisively to the south, as if it had received an urgent summons. The water in the elbow was deep and solemn and quiet; in the summertime it was a good place to fish and swim. Jim watched an oak leaf bump against the rock but catch again in the current; it spun slowly, then continued downstream. He watched it until he lost sight of it in the sunlight glittering on the water.

"Now tell me," Jim said.

"Let me shoot the gun."

"How do I know you won't shoot the gun and then not tell me?"

"Have I ever lied to you?" Dennis Deane asked.

"Well, yes, Dennis Deane. You have. A lot."

"So, I ain't gonna lie to you today."

"Ten shots," Jim said. "That's all."

He handed Dennis Deane the rifle. He searched around in the underbrush until he found a dead limb, which he broke over his knee into several pieces. When he stepped back onto the rock, Dennis Deane levered a shell into the chamber.

"You ready?" Jim asked.

Dennis Deane raised the rifle to his shoulder and squinted down the barrel. "I was born ready," he said.

Jim threw one of the sticks upstream and across the current so that it would pass them on the opposite side of the river from the rock. The first shot Dennis Deane fired at the stick didn't even hit the water, but he immediately levered another shell into the chamber and fired again. This time he managed to hit the water, but nowhere close to the target. As the stick floated past them, Dennis Deane fired the rifle as fast as he could work the lever and pull the trigger. The noise of the shots clapped down the river and echoed back toward them; each of the bullets hit the river with a *thoomp* sound; they sent up small geysers of white water. In between the reports, the spent shell casings bounced off the rock with tiny, almost musical *tinks*. Dennis Deane always shot the rifle as rapidly as possible. No matter how many shells Jim let him shoot, he never made them last.

"Eight," Jim counted. "Nine," he warned. *"Ten."*

By then the stick was perhaps twenty yards downstream, and hard to see in the reflected sunlight. Dennis Deane kept the rifle to his shoulder and squinted harder.

"I said that was ten, Dennis Deane," Jim said. "Don't do it."

Dennis Deane pulled the trigger anyway. The report spat and clapped, and once again the shot seemed to miss the river entirely. The stick bobbed unharmed out of sight. Dennis Deane turned and smiled happily at Jim. A pale string of gun smoke moved out over the water and headed downstream.

"Eleven," Dennis Deane said.

Jim pulled the rifle out of his hands. "Daggummit," he said. "You always do that. You always lie to me. Always."

"Yeah, I know. I don't know why you put up with it."

"Maybe I won't anymore."

"Oh, don't get all huffy."

Jim shook his head.

"How many times did I hit it?"

"None," Jim said. "Two times you didn't even hit the water."

"You're crazy," Dennis Deane said. "I hit that stick eight times. At least."

"You might've hit the river eight times, but that's all. Actually, now that I think about it, you managed to hit the river nine times. But you never got close to the stick."

"Well, if that's how you want to be," Dennis Deane sniffed, "making yourself look big by making other people look small, then go right ahead."

"Don't try to change the subject, Dennis Deane," Jim said.

"What subject?"

"Why are the hillbillies going to kill you?"

The happiness that had come from shooting the rifle slid so quickly and completely out of Dennis Deane's eyes that Jim instantly regretted saying anything.

"Oh, God," Dennis Deane said, "I've got to sit down." He collapsed onto the rock and lay there in the sun with his eyes closed.

Jim stepped off the rock, leaned the rifle carefully against a tree, then returned and sat down beside Dennis Deane.

"What?" he said softly. "What did you do?"

"What's the worst thing in the world you can think of that could happen to you?"

Jim gave the question some thought. "I don't know," he said. "Your mama died?"

"Okay. What's the second-worst thing?"

"You got somebody pregnant?"

Dennis Deane jerked, then turned and stared at Jim, his eyes wide.

"Boy," he said. "You're good."

Jim felt his mouth drop open. "What? You got somebody pregnant?"

"One shot," Dennis Deane said. "Bull's-eye."

"Who?" Jim said. "I mean, *who?*"

"Guess."

"I don't know, Dennis Deane. You don't even have a girlfriend."

"Well, I do now."

"So, who is it?"

Dennis Deane hit his head three times against the rock. (The name was apparently lodged inside his brain and needed to be knocked loose.) But when he opened his mouth, no noise came out.

"You gotta tell me," Jim said.

Dennis Deane swallowed hard and rubbed his throat. When he finally spoke, his voice was barely audible over the sound of the current.

"Ellie Something," he said.

Jim leaned closer to Dennis Deane. "Did you say Ellie Something?"

"Yeah. Ellie Something. You remember that day on the steps before school when I said I could make any girl I wanted to fall in love with me? Well, it actually worked on her."

"You're kidding."

"That's what she told me. I didn't believe it, either."

"And then you got her pregnant?"

"Well, not right then."

"How? I mean, I know *how,* but where? She lives on the mountain and you don't have a car. And she's only a freshman."

"Big Day," Dennis Deane said. "Square dance. And apparently being a freshman doesn't have anything to do with it."

"But you went to the dance with me, and I talked to you in the gym. Where'd you go?"

Dennis Deane closed his eyes again. "Nurse's office."

"The nurse's office, Dennis Deane? You did it in the *nurse's office?*"

"Yep. The nurse's office."

Jim whistled. "Boy," he said. "The nurse's office. Man, you could've been expelled."

"Yeah, that would've been real upsetting," Dennis Deane said. He sat up and wrapped his arms around his knees. "I'm probably not even going to be alive to go to school tomorrow, and all you can worry about is the principal."

"Oh, never mind," Jim said. "You know what I meant."

Both boys sat and stared into the water.

"How come people don't fish in the winter?" Dennis Deane asked.

"What?"

"How come people don't fish in the winter? Today's a pretty nice day. How come people don't go fishing? How come we ain't fishing?"

"Fish don't bite in the winter."

"Don't fish eat in the winter?"

"I don't think so," Jim said.

"What about up north, where people go ice fishing? Those fish must eat."

"I didn't think about that."

"You ever tried it?"

"Tried what?"

"Fishing in the winter."

"Never have. You?"

"Nope. We ought to try it sometime."

"Okay," Jim said. He picked up a twig and flicked it toward the water. "So, what was it like?"

"What was what like?"

"You know, with Ellie Something. What was it like?"

"You don't know what it's like?"

Jim looked away from Dennis Deane. "I guess not. No. Not really."

"Huh," Dennis Deane said. "I always thought that you and Norma, well, that you were doing it and just not telling me."

"Lord, no," Jim said.

"How far'd you get? Third base?"

"Dennis Deane, I really don't want to talk about Norma."

"Second base?"

Jim blushed miserably but didn't reply. His recent, brief trip to second base with Norma didn't feel like anything he should brag about.

"First base?" Dennis Deane said in disbelief. "You dated Norma Harris *all that time* and you only got to first base?"

"Norma didn't like baseball," Jim said. "I don't want to talk about this anymore."

He noticed five pebbles resting in a small, bowl-shaped depression in the face of the rock. He wondered how the river had managed to pick them up when the water was high and deposit them so carefully in this one spot. He tossed them one at a time into the water. Then he stood and collected the shell casings that hadn't rolled off the rock and tossed them into the water as well. Then he sat back down.

"Do you think she's pretty?" Dennis Deane asked.

"Who?"

"Ellie Something."

"I guess so," Jim said. "Do you?"

"I guess I think she's kind of nice to look at. I know she smells good."

"Well, that's something."

"Do you really think she's pretty?"

Jim hadn't thought about Ellie Something one way or another, but he said, "Sure. Ellie Something's a pretty little girl."

"That's good," Dennis Deane said. "At least I didn't get no ugly girl pregnant."

"You never did tell me what it was like."

Dennis Deane frowned. "I don't really know how to explain it," he said. "It was different than I thought."

"Different better or different worse?"

"Just different different. You know how, when you're by yourself and you think about doing it?"

Jim nodded slightly.

"Well, I guess I never really thought about the girl being there."

"How can you think about doing it without thinking about a girl?"

"I mean, sure, you think about a girl being there, but Ellie Something, she was *really* there. You know what I'm saying?"

"No," Jim said.

"Okay, well, sex, I never thought about it being something girls were interested in. I guess I'd always just thought about it being something we did to them. I never thought about it being something they did to us. Does that make any sense?"

Jim pondered a minute. "You mean you're saying Ellie Something did it to you? Is that what you're saying?"

"Not exactly. I guess what I'm saying is that she did it, *too*. And I'd never thought about that before. You think about doing it, but you don't really think about the girl. You don't think about being *with* somebody like that. But then you're doing it for real and you realize that somebody else is there with you and you realize that you've got your britches pulled down and your butt sticking up in the air and they've got their britches pulled down, too, and you feel like you're going someplace together and it's kind of embarrassing, but it's fun at the same time. Although it don't seem that much fun now."

Jim nodded slowly. "Huh," he said.

"Then, there you go. That's what it was like."

"So, what happens now?"

"I don't know, but it ain't going to be good. She was going to tell her mama and daddy today after church. Then I figure they're going to come down here and tell Mama."

"Uh-oh."

"You ain't kidding about uh-oh," Dennis Deane

said. "I figure her daddy's got some kind of hillbilly posse rounded up by now. They're probably waiting for me at the house."

"Do you love her?"

Dennis Deane didn't say anything.

"Hey," Jim said.

"What?"

"Do you love Ellie Something?"

"I guess so. I mean, I think so. I mean I think about her a lot. I didn't used to think about her at all. What does that mean? I look forward to seeing her get off the school bus. Does that mean I love her?"

"As far as I know. Are you going to marry her?"

"Would you?"

"Marry Ellie Something?"

"Not just Ellie Something. Anybody. If you got somebody pregnant, would you marry her?"

Jim closed his eyes. He thought about Chrissie and imagined carrying her over the threshold to his room and laying her down on his bed. He imagined holding a baby with black hair and found that the prospect made him happy. A little girl. He opened his eyes.

"Yeah," he said. "I think I would."

"I figured you'd say that. You always were a goody-goody."

"I don't know what else you could do."

"But I'm too young to get married," Dennis Deane said. "Do you have any idea how immature I am?"

Jim laughed. "Yeah, I think I do. You're pretty dog-gone immature."

"You ain't fooling none there," Dennis Deane said. "I'm the most immature person I know. I'm practically *childish*."

"Are you going to marry her?"

"Yeah, I guess so," Dennis Deane said. "Can I shoot your rifle some more?"

"No."

At a point Jim hadn't noticed, the sun had dropped low enough behind the trees that the light had left the surface of the water. The river had taken on a leaden hue; the water in the elbow had darkened into a color approaching black. Though the tops of the trees still glowed in the flat winter sunlight, the rock on which they sat lay completely in shadow. Jim shivered and buttoned the top button of his coat.

"So, what are you going to do?" Dennis Deane asked.

"About what?"

"About Chrissie."

"Nothing," Jim said. "There's nothing I can do. All I've got to look forward to is graduating so at least I won't have to look at her every day. Maybe she'll move back to Oklahoma to live with Injun Joe and the rest of the Cherokees."

"Or something could happen to Bucky."

"Oh, yeah? Like what?"

"I don't know. You could always shoot him."

"I've thought about it," Jim said. "I probably would if I could get away with it."

Dennis Deane stood and picked up one of the sticks Jim had broken for target practice. "Well, why don't you shoot him?"

Jim stared at the stick in Dennis Deane's hand and started to grin. "Why not?"

"Sure," Dennis Deane said, waving the stick at Jim. "Why not?"

Jim retrieved his rifle from the bank and loaded the tube full of shells. He stepped to the edge of the rock and shouldered it.

"You ready?" Dennis Deane asked.

"Throw it out there."

Dennis Deane tossed the stick into the current on the far side of the river. "There he goes, Jim!" he said. "Don't let him get away!"

Jim sighted down the barrel. The stick turned in the current until it was broadside to the rock. As it nosed downstream, it began to pick up speed. Jim tracked the stick with the rifle and drew a bead on a spot in the middle of it.

"Hey, Bucky," he said. "Over here."

When they left the river, they met Uncle Zeno driving his truck toward them around the edge of the bottom. Uncle Zeno pulled the truck off the farm road and rolled down the passenger-side window.

Jim stopped the Major beside the truck. "What's going on?" he asked.

Uncle Zeno looked grim. "The Japanese just bombed Pearl Harbor," he said.

"What's Pearl Harbor?" Dennis Deane asked.

Bucky Comes Home

JIM HEARD the train stopping along the edge of his dream and, without waking, wondered why. Nothing ever stopped in Aliceville during the middle of the night. Then he heard someone pounding on a door, but he figured he would be okay as long as he didn't open it. He heard heavy footsteps moving toward the door and the rattle of a knob and the creak of a screen on its hinges and the indistinct murmur of two voices, one asking questions, the other answering, the voices speaking urgently, almost on top of each other. The screen creaked again and the door clicked closed and the footsteps — Uncle Zeno's, Jim recognized them now — grew louder as they moved down the hallway through the house in which Jim had begun to remember he lived. He heard Uncle Zeno open Mama's door and speak quickly to her, and he heard Mama throw back her covers. Her shoes scuffed against the floor as she slipped her feet into them. Jim, fully awake now, stared at his door until it opened.

"Get up," Uncle Zeno said.

"What is it?"

"Bucky's here."

Jim squinted at Uncle Zeno's silhouette. The light slanting past it from the kitchen hurt his eyes. "Here?" he said.

"At the depot. Get dressed. They're holding the train for him."

When Jim ran from his room, he passed Mama sitting at the kitchen table, the quilt she had made with Norma draped over her shoulders. Her eyes were red and wide, and she held both hands in front of her mouth. He burst through the screen door and leapt from the top step into the yard. The ground was frozen and his pants slapped icily against his legs as he sprinted beside the waiting train toward the depot. The boxcars, stilled in a place they weren't supposed to be, bore the premonitory oddness of an apparition; from the corner of his eye, as he ran alongside them, they seemed to move silently toward the destination from which they had been kept. The windows of the depot were dark, but Pete Hunt, the station agent, stood on the platform beside a man holding a lantern. Jim slowed and climbed the steps. Pete and the man with the lantern stared at him. He heard himself panting loudly and tried to breathe through his nose. To his left gaped the open door of a boxcar, but he didn't dare look inside it. He smelled wood smoke and wondered who else in town was awake at this hour.

"Jim here played ball with him," Pete said.

"That right?" said the man.

"Yes, sir," Jim said.

"He any good?"

From the street behind him Jim heard footsteps jogging toward the depot. Uncle Zeno had rousted Uncle Coran and Uncle Al. Their change and knives jangled in their pockets as they ran. "He played shortstop," Jim said.

"Best I ever saw," said Pete. "Boy had an arm like a gun."

Jim blinked at Pete. *A gun that couldn't shoot straight,* he thought, and instantly felt ashamed.

The man studied Jim's face. "Too bad," he said.

The uncles clomped onto the platform behind him. Uncle Zeno briefly placed a hand on Jim's shoulder as he walked into the lantern light.

"This ought to do," said the man. "Let's get him off."

Jim fell in behind Uncle Zeno and stepped from the platform across the narrow gap into the car. Uncle Al came in after him. Jim found himself standing alongside Bucky's coffin. Pete and Uncle Coran faced them from the other side of it.

The man stepped into the car last, and when he held the lantern up in the air, their shadows loomed crazily around the walls. "Here's your boy," he said — unnecessarily, Jim thought, because the coffin was the only thing inside the car. It looked like it had been nailed together in a hurry. A bill of lading was tacked to the lid and the word BUCKLAW swam up at

Jim before he looked away. The man placed the lantern on the floor behind him.

"Y'all smell that?" Uncle Al asked.

Jim gagged and put his hand over his mouth and nose.

"He's about ripe," the man said.

Uncle Coran backed up a step and looked around angrily. "Now, damn it," he said. "This ain't right. There ain't nothing right about this." When nobody disagreed with him, he stepped back up to the coffin.

"I kept the doors open the whole way. I tried to freeze him, cold as it is, but I guess it didn't work."

"You gonna make it, Doc?" Uncle Zeno asked.

Jim didn't think so, but he nodded.

"He's lucky he made it back home," the man said. "I heard they only shipped a few. Let's see if we can get him up."

Jim took a deep breath and held it and squatted and tried to work his fingers underneath the casket. He felt the box lift from Uncle Zeno's end, then Uncle Al's.

"Up," said Uncle Zeno.

Jim lifted and stood and the casket swung unevenly into the air. The weight inside it was shocking. It was, well, *dead.*

"I don't have a good grip," Pete said.

"Get one," said Uncle Coran, who stood next to Pete.

Jim realized that the wood beneath his right hand was damp, the wetness slick and icy. "Oh, God," he said.

"I know, Doc," Uncle Zeno said. "Don't drop it."

The six of them began to shuffle sideways toward the door. "Watch your step," the man said.

They carried the coffin to the far end of the platform and carefully put it down, first Jim's side, then the other. Everyone got their fingers out from underneath it intact. They stepped back and looked down at it. Nobody spoke. The man returned to the boxcar and retrieved his lantern and from the platform waved it in a bright arc at his side toward the engine. Jim stared at his right hand and considered wiping it on his pants, but he thought better of it.

Up ahead a bell began to ring lazily in the darkness. Jim heard a determined *chuff* of steam and then another, and the wheels of the engine began a slow, almost animate screech against the rails. As each car began to move, it pulled with a heavy clank against the coupling of the stationary car behind it, dragging its brother, groaning, into reluctant motion. The sound of the individual couplings clanking together galloped in succession away from the engine, car to car to car to car, growing louder as it approached Jim's position on the platform and softer as it ran away; in a second or two it leapt into the darkness beyond the far end of the train. And then the boxcars were moving smoothly, gaining speed, bracketed by thin slashes of darkness. The brightly lit caboose, when it passed, left them alone on the end of the platform in an exposed, unexpected quiet; as it drew abreast of the man with the lantern, he nodded toward them and touched the brim of his cap with his index finger and stepped nimbly onto the rear step of the car. He opened the door, walked inside, and closed it behind him. Jim watched the lighted window of the doorway until it passed out of sight around the bend. And then the train was gone. Jim stood with the uncles and Pete in the starlight on the platform. When the engine whistled at the crossing east of town, it already sounded far away.

Uncle Coran tapped the coffin twice with his toe.

"Now what do we do?" Uncle Al asked.

"I don't know," Pete said. "I can't keep him here. Not with him the way he is."

"We'll take him home," said Uncle Zeno. "Somebody run get the truck."

Jim scrubbed his hands in the kitchen sink until they ached in the cold water. He refused to say anything to Mama about what had happened. He was afraid that if he opened his mouth he would vomit. He changed his pants, even though he hadn't wiped his hands on them, rounded up an armload of old quilts, and ran back to the depot, leaving Mama on the top step, worrying questions into the air behind him. At the depot someone had backed the truck up to the platform, and Pete and the uncles had slid Bucky's coffin onto the bed. Uncle Zeno had tacked scrap pieces of two-by-fours around the base of the coffin to keep it from sliding. Jim hoped he wouldn't have to touch it ever again. Just looking at it made him wish he had scrubbed his hands harder.

"Boys, I'd be glad to at least make you some coffee," Pete said.

"We need to get on up the road," Uncle Zeno said. "Jim, you going with us?"

"Yes, sir."

"Then, who's going to ride in the back?" Uncle Al asked. "We can't all fit up front."

"I will," said Jim. He had shot Bucky. Nobody else knew that.

"You sure?" asked Uncle Zeno.

"Yes, sir. I'll do it."

"All right, then. Let's load up."

Jim walked from the platform onto the truck bed and maneuvered around Bucky's coffin, staying as far away from it as possible. Uncle Zeno stepped on behind Jim, and Jim handed him the quilts. When Jim sat down with his back against the cab and extended his legs, his feet hit the end of the casket. He immediately jerked them back.

"Go ahead and stretch out, Doc," Uncle Zeno said, shaking out and tucking the quilts one at a time around Jim. "You ain't going to bother him."

"Was that a joke?" Jim asked.

"I don't think so. If Bucky was in that box and you were kicking it, then he might raise up and ask you to quit. But Bucky ain't in there."

"Oh, yes, he is."

"No, he's not. What's in that box will be dirt by springtime. You warm enough?"

"I guess so. Not really," Jim said.

"Just stay hunkered down. Maybe Corrie or Allie will switch places with you when we come back down the mountain."

"All right."

"A box can't hold the spirit, Jim. Right now Bucky's sitting around the throne with the rest of those boys. You remember that."

"But I still feel like he's in there."

"People are always looking for ghosts in the grave-yard, Doc. But that's the last place they'd be likely to find one."

"I hope you're right."

Uncle Zeno stepped to the side of the bed and jumped off. "Unh," he said. "Ground's hard."

They drove toward the mountain beneath one of those winter skies that made Jim wonder why he didn't study it more, why he didn't bother to learn when and where the planets made their appearances, and the names of the constellations. So vivid and bright were the stars that the great mechanisms that moved them across the sky seemed almost understandable while remaining incomprehensible, like a familiar Bible story read aloud in a foreign language, or the ticking guts of a watch.

The night was bitterly cold. Jim looked at the stars until the pain of the cold air swirling over his face became unbearable, then he pulled the quilts over his head and breathed into his mittened hands. Eventually he at least stopped shivering. Underneath the quilts, he tried to figure out, through the motion of the truck, exactly where they were on the trip up the mountain, but he lost track soon after they crossed the bridge over Painter Creek. The curves invariably bent opposite to the ways he anticipated. The road fell in the places he imagined it would rise, and rose in the places he was sure it would fall. Several times he tried to think backward and remember the sequence of the curves and hills they had just traversed so he could align the template of his memory atop the map of the road he carried inside his head, yet the two never matched up. Jim could have been anywhere, but he discovered inside that disorientation a small measure of comfort. As long as the road beneath him moved randomly, he found it possible to imagine that its destination remained fluid. He wasn't on his way to the Bucklaws' after all, and the corpse of a boy whose death he had wished for wasn't lying inches from his feet. Bucky didn't even have to be dead. Chrissie and Bucky could get married, for all Jim cared. And when the truck finally stopped and he looked out from beneath the quilts, the war would be over and he wouldn't have to fight in it.

Eventually the growl of the engine withdrew to a great distance. Bucky rode on the front bumper of the truck, draped in a peacoat and holding on to his sailor hat, but he was too far away to worry about. Someone wearing mittens tenderly cradled Jim's face. He leaned into the hands, and breathed on them to keep them warm, and rubbed his cheeks against the scratchy wool.

"That feels nice," Chrissie said. "Your face is warm."

"I love you so much," Jim said.

"Oh, I love you, too, Jim. But do you know the answer?"

"What answer?"

"To number twelve."

"I didn't know we had any homework."

"It's due tomorrow, Jim. Now I have to go ask somebody else."

"No, wait," Jim said. "Don't go. I bet I can figure it out. Tell me the problem."

"Okay. There's these two trains," Chrissie said. "And they're going two different directions. We have to calculate the area."

"Of the trains?"

"Yes. It's a train problem."

"Are you sure you don't mean the volume? If you told me the dimensions of the cars and how many there were, I bet I could figure out the volume."

"No. The book says area."

"But I don't know how to do that," Jim said. "How do you calculate the area of a train? It's a three-dimensional object. Do you mean surface area, or what?"

"You're going to get us in trouble."

"No, I just want to marry you."

"I want to marry you, too, Jim, but you know I can't."

"Why not? We can ask Norma for the answer."

"No. Look what's behind us."

Jim lowered the quilt and peeked out over the top. He saw Bucky Bucklaw running easily in the distance behind the truck. His body looked solid, but it seemed to be made out of darkness. And as Bucky ran, the darkness peeled away in sheets, like ashes, or gauze, and caught the wind and billowed out in shreds behind him.

Jim pushed himself hard against the cab of the truck. He pulled the quilts up over his face but could still see Bucky running along the starlit road. And Bucky must have seen Jim watching him, because he waved and sped up and flew toward the truck until he was within arm's length of the bed.

"No!" Jim yelled. "Get away! Get away from me, Bucky. I'm not kidding around."

The darkness peeling off Bucky made a flapping sound, like newspaper, as the wind whipped it away. Jim hoped that Bucky would eventually blow away and disappear, but he didn't seem to be getting any smaller.

"What's the matter, old buddy?" Bucky asked. "Are you scared? Are you scared of me, now that I'm back?"

"I ain't scared of you," Jim lied. "I just want you to get away from me. That's all."

"Are you going to my house?"

"No. We're not going to your house."

"You are, too."

"No, we're not. I don't even know where your house is. We're going somewhere else."

"Where?"

"Somewhere. I don't know where. I'm not driving the truck."

Bucky laughed and pointed at Jim. "You're lying to me, you old hound dog. You are, too, going to my place. Hey. Watch this." He ripped a swatch of darkness about the size of a handkerchief off his left arm and held it up and let it go in the breeze. "Woo-hoo!" he yelled. "Did you see that? I've been doing that all night."

"Please go away, Bucky," Jim said. "I'll leave Chrissie alone. I promise I will."

Bucky leaned forward and placed both palms flat against the truck bed. "It's a little late for that, old buddy," he whispered. "There's a ladder in the well. Ask Daddy about it when you get there."

The truck started up the first steep grade of the mountain, and Jim tipped to one side and pitched forward and hit something solid with his shoulder. He knew instantly that it was Bucky's coffin, and that he would have to fight Bucky because he had collided with it. Bucky shouted and flew into the truck bed and covered Jim so thoroughly with darkness that Jim could neither breathe nor see. Jim screamed and punched and kicked but got tangled up and couldn't free himself.

"Get off!" Jim yelled, thrashing wildly. "Get off me, Bucky. I'll kill you! I swear to God, I'll kill you if you don't get off me!"

Then the darkness tore away around him, and Bucky's spirit exploded into a blast of angry, frigid air, leaving Jim on his knees searching for it in the quilts. He had killed Bucky all over again, and again wanted to bring him back. The truck stopped suddenly, sliding briefly on the gravel, and Jim rolled against the cab, banging his head. He grabbed it with both hands and curled up in a ball.

"Please leave me alone," he whimpered. "I didn't really want you to die."

"Jim!" somebody yelled. "Hey! Jim!"

Jim opened his eyes and saw the head and shoulders of a dark figure on the running board of the truck, looking at him around the back of the cab. For a second he thought Bucky had come back to fight him some more, but then he recognized Uncle Al.

"What the hell's wrong with you?" Uncle Al asked.

Jim sat up and looked warily at the coffin. He realized he was freezing and wrapped his arms around his knees. He began looking around, trying to figure out what had happened to the quilts.

"Bucky," he said. "Bucky was in here with me, and we were fighting."

"You say you were fighting with Bucky?"

"Yes, sir," Jim said.

Uncle Al glanced at the coffin before disappearing into the cab. Jim heard him say, "He says he was fighting with Bucky."

Uncle Zeno climbed out the other door and looked around the back of the cab. "You say Bucky was back there with you?"

"Yes, sir, but I guess it was just a bad dream."

"I reckon it was. What did he say?"

"I don't remember. He told me to leave Chrissie alone."

"Sounds like a guilty conscience to me," Uncle Al said.

"There's nothing wrong with my conscience," Jim said. "I haven't laid a hand on that girl."

"You want to ride up here with us?" Uncle Zeno asked.

Jim stood and began sorting out the quilts. "No, sir," he said.

Uncle Coran's head appeared beside Uncle Al's. "I'll ride back there, Jim," he said. "I ain't scared of no knothead ghost."

"You'd be afraid of this one," Jim said.

The uncles were quiet for a moment or two. "All right, Doc," Uncle Zeno finally said. "You get covered up again and we'll finish this job."

The Red Canoe

$\mathcal{J}$IM DIDN'T go to sleep again the rest of the way up the mountain. He closely watched the road unrolling behind the truck and kept a wary eye on the woods in the dark places where the trees grew closest to the right-of-way, but he didn't see Bucky again. The fact that Bucky did not haunt Jim while Jim was awake more or less convinced him that he had dreamed the whole thing. The dream, however, seemed more real to him than anything he could think of that he knew for certain had actually happened. He tried to pull the quilts more tightly around himself, and he wondered if a ghost who appeared in a dream was considered a real ghost, or if you had to be awake when you saw it in order for it to count. Ghost or dream, Bucky had at least been on his way home, a destination Jim found hard to hold against him. Jim was quite sure that when he died, home was the one place, aside from heaven, he would want to go. He tried to tell himself that any ghost who would run all the way from Hawaii just to get back to North Carolina couldn't be all bad.

Once the road climbed through the switchbacks and into the valley at the top of the mountain, Jim noticed that most of the stars had dimmed to the point where he could no longer see them and that the sky had begun to brighten into the noncolor of the day when it's still deciding what it wants to be. Up the narrow tracks that climbed into the hollows Jim occasionally spied the sleepy glow of a kerosene lamp burning in a kitchen window. A solitary planet remained lit low in the sky and he found himself wondering if God had forgotten to blow it out. He wished once again that he knew enough about the stars and planets to say, Look, Chrissie, there's Jupiter, or Mars, or whatever it was, but he also knew, now that daylight was almost here, that he wasn't so interested in astronomy that he would go to the necessary trouble of learning about it. Many Varmints Eat Much Juice Saturday Unless Nobody Pays was the sentence Norma had come up with in eighth grade to help them memorize the names and orbits of the planets, and that was probably all he would ever know about the subject. Norma had recently gotten her hands on an old college calculus book and studied it at home for no other reason than that she loved math. Jim couldn't think of anything, other than Chrissie, that he cared about that much.

Uncle Zeno turned off the headlights around the

time they passed Penn's house, and by the time they reached the Bucklaw place, the first rays of new sunlight had climbed out of the valley, casting long, tentative shadows against the mountainside. Nothing in the landscape suggested that bad news had recently arrived here, or would ever come. The orchards rolled away from the farm road in prosperous formation, ridge after terraced ridge, all the way to the top of the mountain. The grass was combed white with frost. The fruit trees glittered like fountains whose water had sprung suddenly from the earth, only to freeze before it touched the ground. Jim began to wonder about Bucky's parents. How could anyone who lived looking onto a scene so precisely beautiful even imagine they might one morning see a strange truck coming up the road with their son's body laid out in the back? Uncle Coran had been right. None of this made any sense. Jim gently nudged the coffin with the toe of one boot. "Hey. Wake up, Bucky," he said. "You're home."

As they approached the house, Jim spotted the two German shepherds who had attacked his car back in the fall silently streaking toward the truck, their ears up, their bushy tails straight out behind them. He scrambled to his feet and threw his arms over the cab, ready to climb onto the roof. But when the dogs drew close they yelped and pulled up before reaching the road. They trotted in small, tight circles, their tails between their legs and bellies low to the ground, before loping away at an angle, looking back over their shoulders. Only later would Jim realize that the smell had stopped them.

The house was two stories tall, constructed of quartz fieldstone Bucklaw Sr. had pulled out of his orchards when he moved to this side of the mountain and cut away the timber. After all these years, the rocks still bore the orange color of the dirt from which they had been dug. In the yard, Uncle Zeno stopped the truck and blew the horn. Jim caught a glimpse of Chrissie wearing a white nightgown, framed in an upstairs window. He moved his hand to wave at her, but she disappeared so quickly he had the fleeting notion that she must be dead, too. Before he had time to wonder what she was doing here, the front door opened and Bucky's father stepped onto the porch. Mr. Bucklaw put on his hat and adjusted the brim and closed the door behind him. He stared for a long moment at the truck, his face expressionless, his breath billowing evenly from his nostrils in quick white snorts. Jim thought, *He's going to blame me*, and fought the urge to leap down and run.

Mr. Bucklaw came slowly down the stairs, never taking his eyes from the bed of the truck, and took four steps into the yard before he crumpled at the waist. He dropped to his knees and wrenched his hat from his head and began slapping the back of his neck with it. Jim held his hands over his ears. The uncles scrambled out of the cab and rushed to Mr. Bucklaw and pulled him to his feet. Uncle Zeno and Uncle Coran wrapped their arms around him so that he couldn't hit himself anymore, and Uncle Zeno crooned the same wordless, soothing noises he might have made to a spooked animal. Uncle Al worked the crumpled hat from out of Mr. Bucklaw's fingers. He looked down at the hat, then around for somewhere to put it; he tried to mold it back into shape before finally giving up and holding it awkwardly in front of himself, crown down, like an usher passing a collection plate. Jim jumped down from the truck but gave the uncles and Mr. Bucklaw a wide berth.

Only the uncles holding Mr. Bucklaw kept him from collapsing again onto the ground. "Ohh," he moaned. "Oh, sweet Jesus. I can't do this."

"Let's get him to the house," said Uncle Zeno.

The toes of Mr. Bucklaw's boots dragged the ground as Uncle Zeno and Uncle Coran helped him away from the truck. At the house the uncles lowered him onto the second step. He leaned forward until his chest rested on his thighs. "It's too hard," he said. "I just can't do this. It's too hard."

Uncle Zeno and Uncle Coran sat down on either side of him, without touching him. Uncle Al extended Mr. Bucklaw's hat. Mr. Bucklaw took it and flung it into the yard, almost hitting Uncle Al with the hat and Uncle Zeno with his arm. Uncle Al didn't go get it.

"I don't understand," Mr. Bucklaw said. "Where did you find him? How did you end up with him? All we got is the telegram they sent us. They ain't said nothing about when he was supposed to come home."

"He came on the train last night," Uncle Zeno said.

"The stationmaster got us up because we live right there. Nobody's sure where he came from."

"I would have come and got him," Mr. Bucklaw said. "He's my boy. I got a truck. I would have come and got him."

"We didn't think you ought to have to do that," Uncle Zeno said quietly.

Mr. Bucklaw rose upright and gaped at Uncle Zeno. "What am I saying?" he said. "You came all this way. You came all this way and it dark and brought Bucky home. I thank you. I'm sorry I didn't say that sooner."

The uncles all turned away. Jim rolled a small stick back and forth with his toe.

"Now what do I do?" Mr. Bucklaw asked. He gazed almost eagerly into each of the uncles' faces. "I don't know what I'm supposed to do."

Uncle Zeno spoke as softly as Jim had ever heard him. "You need to put him somewhere," he said.

"Put him somewhere," said Mr. Bucklaw. "I need to put him somewhere."

"Tell us where," said Uncle Coran.

Mr. Bucklaw looked blankly around the yard before pointing slowly up the steps. "In the house," he said. "I guess we ought to put him in the house."

"We might need to stop and think here for a minute," Uncle Zeno said.

"What?"

"He's not in too good a shape," said Uncle Zeno. "The body's not. You may not want to put him inside just yet."

"Oh, God," Mr. Bucklaw said. "Please don't tell me that." He tilted slowly, then listed and fell sideways onto Uncle Zeno. He began to cry with his face mashed against Uncle Zeno's arm. Uncle Coran took him by the shoulders and guided him back to vertical.

"Maybe we ought to put him on the porch for now," Uncle Zeno said. "I bet he would like it out here on the porch, where he could see."

"Oh, Jesus," Mr. Bucklaw sobbed. "The porch. I don't know. I don't know what I'm supposed to do."

The front door opened and Chrissie stepped outside. She was wearing Bucky's Aliceville letter jacket. Uncle Coran stood up and took off his hat.

"Side porch," she said to Uncle Zeno. "We'll put him on the side porch for now."

Mr. Bucklaw reached toward her. "Chrissie, I don't know what to do," he said.

"You need to come on inside, Mr. Bucklaw," she said. "You need to come inside and go see Mrs. Bucklaw. We'll take care of things out here."

Mr. Bucklaw nodded. Uncle Zeno and Uncle Coran lifted him to his feet. "That's Bucky's fiancée," he said.

"We're sorry for your loss, Miss Steppe," Uncle Zeno said, removing his hat. Chrissie nodded. Uncle Al cleared his throat and went after Mr. Bucklaw's hat.

"She's been staying with us and helping Mama," Mr. Bucklaw said, starting heavily up the stairs. "Chrissie, is Mama all right?"

"No, sir," Chrissie said. "She's not all right. She

looked out the window and saw who it was. You need to go upstairs."

Mr. Bucklaw left the door standing open behind him. Chrissie closed it, then walked to the edge of the porch and studied the truck. She bit her lower lip.

"Things haven't been too good here," she said.

"Here's his hat," said Uncle Al, handing it up.

"Thank you."

"What do you want us to do?" Uncle Zeno asked.

"Sawhorses," Chrissie said. "I guess we're going to need sawhorses."

"Jim will go get the sawhorses," Uncle Zeno said. "Where do y'all keep them?"

"Wood shop," Chrissie said, pointing back down the road. "Between the first barn and the big packing shed."

"Go get two sawhorses, Jim," said Uncle Zeno.

The wood shop was a simple frame building, sided with corrugated metal and open at one end. Just inside the opening sat a single worn-looking, split-bottomed chair, its legs half buried in wood shavings. A lantern was suspended from the rafter above it with a piece of baling wire. Hammers and mallets and saws and wood chisels and files hung neatly above a workbench at the opposite end. Another lantern hung above the bench. Along the wall to Jim's right a red canvas canoe rested on the sawhorses he had been sent to find. He drew his finger along the brightly varnished side of the canoe and looked inside. The frame was made of bent and polished ash, as gracefully formed and light-looking as the skeleton of a bird. The seats were woven of narrow oak splits into an intricate diamond pattern.

"Bucky built that," a voice said behind him.

Jim started at the voice, and again at the figure silhouetted by the white winter sunlight.

"I didn't mean to scare you," Chrissie said. She stepped into the building and off to the side, out of the glare.

"I thought you were somebody else," Jim said.

She wasn't wearing Bucky's letter jacket any longer but had on the plaid cloth coat she normally wore to school.

"It was hanging by the door," she said.

"What was?"

"Bucky's letter jacket. It was hanging by the door and I just put it on when I came outside. I was in a hurry."

"I didn't notice."

"Yes, you did."

"Okay, I did. But how did you know what I was thinking?"

"It wasn't hard. You wouldn't make a very good liar."

"So, what am I thinking now?"

Chrissie leaned forward and squinted slightly. "You're thinking, 'I don't care what she wears. She can wear whatever coat she wants to.'"

"That's pretty close," he said. He enjoyed a passing but powerful urge to kick wood chips at her. "You didn't tell me you and Bucky were getting married."

"I'm not exactly Bucky's — I mean, I wasn't — Bucky's fiancée."

"What does that mean? 'Not exactly'?"

"It means I kind of got promoted after Pearl Harbor."

"Well, you live in a nice house now," Jim said. "Congratulations."

"You think I like living here?"

"I don't know. Do you?"

"These poor people loved Bucky, Jim. Now they're just about crazy."

"I understand that part."

"Mrs. Bucklaw says she wants me around because Bucky loved me, but she's got me cooking and cleaning like a maid, except she ain't paying me. And that's about the sanest thing that's going on. I can't wait to get out of that house. It's too sad and strange."

"Did Bucky love you?"

"What? I don't know. I guess. He said he did."

"Did you love him?"

"I think we've already had this conversation."

"Do you miss him?"

"I'm just real sad about everything. I'm afraid he suffered. I'm afraid he was trapped in a fire and he couldn't get out and he knew what was happening. I can't go to sleep for thinking about it. And I'm afraid he's in the house. I'm afraid I'm going to see him coming in the door if I open my eyes. I know you hated him, Jim, but he didn't deserve what happened to him."

"No," Jim said. "You're right. He didn't."

Chrissie stepped closer. "He finished that canoe right before we moved back here. He said it took him almost a year."

"It's beautiful," Jim said, meaning it. "I don't think I could ever make anything like that."

"He said he wanted to cover it in birch bark, but the only birch trees he could find up here were too scrawny."

"Birch bark?"

"Bucky loved boats," Chrissie said. "And he loved Indians."

"Seems like I've heard that before."

"Don't be smart. There's a whole shelf full of books about Indians in his room that he studied long before he ever laid eyes on me. He was one of those white boys who liked to run around in the woods wearing moccasins. Did you ever do that?"

"Not much," Jim said. "I was usually a cowboy."

"Because you like to win?"

"No, because I had a cowboy hat and a pony. Why did you call Bucky a white boy?"

"Because he was."

"But you're half white."

"That depends on whether or not somebody's asking me to mop." Jim opened his mouth to speak, but

Chrissie held up her hand. "I can tell you're about to show your ignorance, Jim, and I'd just as soon you didn't."

"Your mama's white," Jim said.

"There. You went ahead and did it, anyway."

"What did I say?"

"Lift up that end of the canoe," Chrissie said. "We need to get these sawhorses to the house."

They walked slowly along the farm road through the orchards. Jim carried the stacked sawhorses over his shoulder. Chrissie didn't seem in a hurry to get back to the house. The morning was cold but calm, the sunlight weak but bright. It should have been a better day than it was.

"What's been going on at school?" Chrissie asked.

"Everybody's been talking about Bucky and the war. Horace Gentine and Buster Burnette have already joined the navy and gone off to basic training."

"I heard about it."

"We had assembly and prayer meeting every morning for Bucky because they didn't know if he was dead or not. At first it was just preachers coming in, but then kids started asking Mr. Dunlap if they could pray. The day school let out for Christmas, second period was almost over before everybody finished. There's a kid in the fifth grade who says he's called to preach, and I thought they were going to have to drag him off the stage."

"Did you pray for him?"

"No. I mean, not out loud. Everybody was looking at me to see if I would do it."

"But you did pray for him?"

"Yes," Jim said. "When I was by myself. After you told me that day why you couldn't go out with me, I started wishing that Bucky would die."

"Oh, no."

"And Pearl Harbor Day, before we heard, I was down at the river with Dennis Deane shooting my rifle, and I pretended to shoot him."

"That's awful, Jim."

"I know it is," Jim said. "I've been praying about it, but I don't feel much better."

"Maybe we'll all feel better one of these days."

"Maybe." He moved the sawhorses to the other shoulder. "Tell me something. I know you believe in spirits, but do you believe in ghosts?"

"Sometimes spirits can be ghosts," Chrissie said carefully. "And sometimes they're just spirits."

"What would you say if I told you I think I saw Bucky last night?"

Chrissie didn't stop walking, but Jim heard her inhale sharply. "I think I heard him coming up the stairs, but I was too scared to look," she said. "When did you see him?"

"Coming up here. I guess I went to sleep in the truck, and I dreamed he was running up the mountain behind us."

"Did he say anything?"

"He told me to stay away from you."

The corners of Chrissie's mouth flinched upward. "Well, that sounds like him."

"He said there was a ladder in the well. Does that mean anything to you?"

"The Bucklaws have got a pump, so I don't know if there's a ladder down in the well or not. I ain't going to slide the slab back and look, though."

"If Bucky had made it home, what do you think you would have done?"

"I don't know. I guess I would have married him," she said.

Jim thought then of Bucky guiding his red canoe down the river. It was warm, Indian summer, the woods yellow. Chrissie sat in the bow. Jim stood on the flat rock. The water was green and smooth. The canoe was going very fast. Bucky was taking her away from him forever. *Hey, Bucky. Over here.*

"I can't believe you," he said.

"Don't you start on me, Jim. Not today."

"I can't believe you would marry somebody you didn't love."

"I keep telling you, you don't know anything about me."

"I know about Injun Joe," he said. "I know he robbed a bank and shot a cop and you don't even know where he is."

Chrissie stopped and wheeled on Jim. She was crying now. "What did you just call my daddy?" she asked.

He watched a tear drop onto the front of her coat and sink darkly into the wool. He felt as if he had strayed too far in front of the line during a rabbit hunt. If he flushed a rabbit now, somebody was going to shoot him.

"Injun Joe," he said.

And there went the rabbit.

"That's it, Jim Glass," she said. "That's it. You just settled everything."

"Oh, yeah? Then, why did you even come down here just now?"

Chrissie pointed back the way they had come. "Look down there."

Bucky's German shepherds stood about twenty paces behind them, ears up, one in each track of the farm road. They were staring straight at Jim.

"I should have let them eat you," Chrissie said.

February 8, 1942

Lynn's Mountain, NC
Dear Zeno,
  Well, it is a new year here as it is there, and I hope it is better than the last one, although it does not seem that the war news will be good anytime soon and you have to wonder what is happening in the world. I know you must not consider getting a letter from me to be good news either, as it hasn't been in the past, nor have telegrams, and if you think I am writing to you today to ask you for something, then you are right, I'm afraid. Here it is. I have heard that Mr. Harris is going to be looking for somebody to cook and clean at his hotel, and I am writing to see if you would put in a good word for me for the job, as I need it. (You know for yourself that I am a good cook! And I'm still not afraid to work.) We are nothing more than a hardship and a worry up here on Mama and Daddy, who do not have anything other than the scraps the Bucklaws throw them, and besides, I need to get Chrissie away from Mrs. B. because she has not been right since Pearl Harbor and especially since the funeral and she is treating Chrissie like her daughter, but if Mrs. B. had a daughter, she wouldn't make her cook and clean all the time and not pay her. She has got her sleeping in the little room across the hall from Bucky's room and Chrissie does not get a wink of sleep because she says she hears Bucky going up and down the stairs in the dark all night, and I know you don't believe in spooks but I'm not going to say she is wrong, because many places on this

mountain are haunted, as I know you have heard, because you hated riding that mule down the mountain in the dark! I am afraid that they are going to take her away from me. That is why I want to be a cook in the hotel. I have to figure that we will not see Joe again, and if he is not dead already, then they will sentence him to life in prison in Oklahoma for what he did when they catch him, which they will sooner or later, and now I have to figure out how to take care of the two of us without making her feel bad for taking more charity than we have already took. I am not asking you for charity this time, though, only a kind word in passing between two business men in the same town. (I know that your Jim used to go with Mr. Harris' Norma, so I hope he is not feuding with you!) I know you must think I am like an old dog following you around who you cannot run off even if you throw a stick and a rock at it, but I hope this is the last time I will ever have to ask you for anything or anybody else. Cooking and cleaning in a hotel for traveling men is not the job I would have picked out for myself but I made my bed a long time ago when I was young and silly and now I have to lie in it. (That sounds like a joke because I would be making up beds in the hotel but I did not mean for it to be!) It is honest work and Chrissie can stay with me in the cook's room and help me in the kitchen but not upstairs, as I will not let her go there or in the dining room or out on the porch, and I will be able to take care of us, and that is all I want anymore in this life and it is enough. Thank you for anything you might say to Mr. Harris about me, and if you don't choose to, I already understand because I know I don't *deserve it, but Chrissie does. If I get the job and see you on the street I will say howdy but that is all, so you don't have to worry about that. I am as always*

Fondly,
Nancy McAbee Steppe

The Girl on the Bridge

THE FIRST Sunday in March, Mama and Norma decided to give the quilt and a basket of food to Dennis Deane and Ellie Something as a housewarming present. Mama asked Jim to carry them over to Allendale, but Jim didn't want to go. Sure, he wanted to see the mill where Dennis Deane worked and catch up on things, but he didn't want to get anywhere near Ellie Something. She might be showing by now, and just the thought of her being pregnant made his face hot. He had never talked to a pregnant girl before, not that he knew about, and he had no idea where he was supposed to look. How could you possibly be in a room with a pregnant girl and *not* look? And he also remembered Dennis Deane telling him years ago that when girls got pregnant their breasts grew gigantic. If, by some miracle, he managed to avoid looking at Ellie Something's big belly, he figured there was no way in the world he could also avoid looking at her big breasts.

Ultimately, he went along just for the chance to

drive his car. Once the war started, Jim had had no choice but to park the Major. He wasn't happy about it, of course, but saw no way to circumvent it, or even complain about it, without seeming small. The last thing in the world he needed was for someone to see him driving around and throw Bucky's sacrifice in his face. Jim already had enough problems.

While Chrissie now spent weeknights with her mother at the hotel, and he occasionally saw her around town, the unwritten rules against speaking to her seemed only to have grown more restrictive since Bucky's death. The simple fact that he had even wanted to date the so-called fiancée of the fallen hero had somehow called his patriotism into question; somehow once being lined up *against* Bucky had automatically made him *for* the Japanese. So he had dropped the key to the Major into Uncle Zeno's hand without complaint. There was a war on, after all, and he couldn't drive without gasoline, simple as that. But Mama, who never went anywhere, had registered for *her* ration — just in case of emergency, she said, and giving a quilt to Dennis Deane and Ellie Something apparently qualified. Allendale was a fifteen- or sixteen-mile round-trip and Jim was tired of walking or riding a mule everywhere he went. So he agreed to drive. Mama sprang for two gallons of gas.

Jim checked the Major's oil and the air pressure in the tires, and he parked the car in front of the house. He thought about leaving the motor running, because it had been slow to start, but figured that at least one of the uncles would get all over him for wasting gasoline. So he cut the engine and went inside, where he found Mama and Norma working furiously on the quilt, which they had unwrapped and spread out on Mama's bed.

Mama, looking down her nose through her sewing glasses, was busy with her seam ripper, removing the scrap of blue chambray that had once belonged to the shirt owned by Jim's father, while Norma, perched on the side of the bed, whipped two small doorways onto a replacement piece cut from one of Uncle Zeno's red bandanas. Norma looked up and smiled brightly when Jim walked in. He was glad she didn't hate him anymore. He still didn't want to marry her, and never would, but at least now he hoped he would always know her. Mama simply looked sheepish.

"Oh, Norma," she said. "I am so sorry about this. I hope you don't mind me ripping this out." She lifted the piece of chambray away from the quilt and waved it feebly. "And look at it. It's just a scrap. I feel silly."

Norma hopped down from the bed and handed Mama the new red wall of the house. "There's nothing to feel silly about, Elizabeth," she said. "I know what that shirt meant to you."

Jim's nose wrinkled involuntarily, the way it always did when he heard Norma call Mama "Elizabeth." The uncles, and virtually everyone else in town, called her Cissy. Only Norma used Mama's given name.

Mama pinned the new piece against the dark blue background and tilted her head. "It's already a bit faded," she said. "It makes the neighborhood look a little trashy, but I guess it will have to do."

She and Norma threaded needles and, working shoulder to shoulder, began stitching the house back together. "It's funny I'm being so ungenerous about that piece," Mama said. "Jim, my husband, would have given us the shirt if we'd asked for it."

"Mmm?" Norma said. She was holding a straight pin between her lips.

"He was a kind boy," Mama said. "It seems so strange to me now to realize that he was only a boy the whole time I knew him. He was only twenty-three when he died."

Norma took the pin out of her mouth and jammed it into the cushion. "What else was he like?" she asked.

Mama glanced up and stared out the window, her needle poised in midair, the white thread taut beneath it, as if she was expecting her husband any minute.

"He was quiet," she said. "A little shy. He had a lovely singing voice, but you had to stand close to him to hear it. Not like my brothers — they're vain as peacocks about their singing and try to outdo each other until you can't hear anything else — but just a pretty voice, the kind that's pleasant to listen to in the evening. He sang all those old sad mountain songs that go on forever, like 'Barbie Allen.'"

"That sounds nice," Norma said.

"I don't know if I appreciated it enough at the time," said Mama. "He never sang directly to me, of course.

He would have found that too embarrassing. But he would sing when he knew I could hear him, and I wouldn't let on that I had listened."

Norma raised her eyebrows at Jim, but Jim pretended he didn't see her.

"And on Sunday afternoons, especially cold ones like today — this was after we were married and lived in that little tenant house — he would make me pies. His mother was sick a lot when he was little, and he learned how to cook for her. He made better biscuits than I did. He didn't use as much baking soda. My biscuits are pretty to look at, fluffy and all, but I've always suspected they were a little bitter."

"I like your biscuits," Norma said. "Mine are too hard and they tend to burn on the bottom."

"Poor boy," Mama said. "The uncles kidded him unmercifully about those pies."

Jim rattled the change in his pocket. "Are y'all ready to go?" he asked.

"Hold your horses, mister," Mama said. "We still have to quilt the new piece, but that shouldn't take long. You didn't leave the motor running, did you?"

The sky was low and gray and hard-looking — not the roiled, booming sky of early spring, but the bitter, set face of deep winter. A cutting wind from the west chased trash from the fields across the road and occasionally dashed a thimbleful of sleet against the windshield of the Major. Jim drove with his mittens on and the flaps down on his hunting cap. Mama and

Norma peered from above their scarves and turned-up coat collars like wary box turtles. In a week or two the trees would bud and the daffodils would bloom, but all that still seemed months, or even years, away. At least it wouldn't snow. Snow in Jim's part of the world always moved quietly up out of the south, and it was never this cold when it came.

"Who's that on the bridge?" Mama asked.

Jim had already identified the plaid coat and the long black hair blowing wildly below a red knit cap and scarf.

"That's Chrissie Steppe," Norma said. "Where in the world is she going?"

Mama clucked her tongue. "Why, she'll freeze to death."

"We have to give her a ride," Jim said.

"Where's she going to sit?" Norma asked.

"In somebody's lap, I guess," said Jim.

"And I suppose you want it to be yours."

"I'm *driving*, Norma."

"Y'all hush," Mama said. "We at least have to stop and see about her."

The steel bridge over the river was a single lane wide. When they drove onto it, Chrissie moved as close to the guardrail as possible, then looked over her shoulder and recognized the car. She was carrying a package wrapped in newspaper but tied with a fresh-looking white ribbon. Below the hem of her coat her skirt flapped around her bare legs, but at least she had on gloves. She waved by lifting the fingers of one hand from the package. Jim pulled off his hunting cap and shoved it into his coat pocket and stopped the Major beside her. Mama rolled down the window. Chrissie leaned over and looked inside, from face to face to face. As she studied them, only her eyes were visible above her scarf and beneath her cap. Jim could hear one of the guy wires on the bridge banging in the wind.

"Hello," Mama said. "Where are you off to on such a terrible day?"

"Allendale," Chrissie said, pushing her scarf down beneath her chin. "I've been meaning to get over to see Ellie and this is the first chance I've had."

"That's five more miles," Jim said.

"I'm hoping that once I get there, they'll know somebody headed back this way."

"It's a small world," Mama said. "That's where we're headed. To see the newlyweds. Why don't you ride with us?"

Chrissie considered the crowded front seat, and Jim saw the shadow of some mischievous, secret thought peering out through her dark pupils. With a finger she brushed a strand of hair away from her mouth.

"I couldn't," she said. "Y'all don't have room."

"Sure we do," Mama said. "Jim's going to ride in the rumble seat."

"I am?" Jim said. "But who's going to drive the Major?"

Mama giggled as she opened her door. "*I* am. Hop out. We'll let you use the quilt, won't we, Norma?"

Jim took the long way around the front of the car so he would have to walk by Chrissie on his way to the rumble seat. Mama shoved the quilt at him when she passed him on her way to the driver's side. She knew what he was up to.

Chrissie had to push the passenger-side door closed to make room between the car and the guardrail for Jim to get by. Jim stopped in front of her. There wasn't much room.

"Thank you for doing this," she said. "I was about to turn around."

"You're welcome," Jim said. "I'm glad to."

She looked down at the box in the crook of her arm. "It's just a cookie jar," she said. "It looks like a cat. Its head is the lid." She shielded her mouth with her free hand. "It was made in *Japan*."

Jim held up the quilt. "Mama and Norma pieced this for Ellie and Dennis Deane. It was made in Aliceville." He tried smiling at her.

She shook her head. "You know I'm still mad at you."

"I know."

"I expected better."

"Yeah. Me, too."

She frowned a little, looking at him. "Do you want my cap?" she asked. "It's awful cold."

It was obviously a girl's cap — it had snowflakes and happy snowmen knitted into it — but Jim nodded stupidly, hoping the bill of his hunting cap wasn't sticking out of his coat pocket.

"Thank you," he said. "That would be a help."

When Chrissie pulled off her cap and handed it to Jim, her hair popped with static electricity and began to levitate in the wind. She tried, with no discernible success, to pat it back down.

"I better get in," she said.

Jim plopped down into the rumble seat, pulled his hunting cap out of his pocket, and dropped it onto the floorboard. He looked over the side of the bridge. The river was dark and swift, metallic-looking, almost silent beneath the whip and yowl of the wind. He winced as Mama ground the gears, looking for first. The car bucked twice, then moved steadily forward and off the bridge. Jim pulled the quilt up over his head and — once hidden from view — Chrissie's cap down over his face.

Mill Hill

*A*s the Major began to descend the steep hill across the river from Allendale, Jim pushed Chrissie's cap above his eyes and lowered the quilt from his face. The white, uniform houses of the mill village clung to the hillside opposite, strung together along muddy streets. Below the houses lay the ornate WPA bridge, complete with wrought-iron lampposts, that spanned the river and connected the two hills. The river here had been backed into near stillness by a dam wedged into the gorge downstream, and the four-story mill building loomed over the water as if studying its reflection. The mill's opaque windows glowed against the dim afternoon, although here and there black windowpanes lurked mysteriously among the mostly silver-painted glass. Slightly distorted by the otherwise imperceptible movement of the river, the reflection struck Jim as belonging to a structure grander than the cotton mill running a full Sunday shift that actually produced it — a citadel guarding an ancient port against Barbary pirates, or a castle in a brightly colored book, a jolly king raising a toast to his knights in the banquet hall.

As they crossed the bridge, the anxiety Jim had always felt as a baseball player entering Allendale to play the Spinners began reflexively buzzing in his gut. Allendale High had always whipped Aliceville School unmercifully, and — though he would never have admitted it — Jim suspected it was because boys who grew up in mill towns were simply tougher than boys who grew up farming. If you ever got a hit against Allendale, you knew that the next time you batted, the pitcher would try to stick one in your ear. Teams that managed to beat the Allendale nine routinely had to fight their way off the field and — if the game was played in Allendale — all the way to the bus. Jim figured that the only good thing to come from the school board's decision to cancel the baseball season was not having to face Allendale. He of course hated himself a little for being afraid of another baseball team, and for worrying that one of the lintheads from the dance might recognize him. When Mama downshifted into first for the pull up Mill Hill, the straining note of the Major's engine struck his ear as puny.

During the summer, when its houses were partially shaded by the chinaberry and locust trees that had found purchase on the hillside, Allendale, at least from a distance, presented to the world a face of superficial loveliness. But when the leaves were off the trees, as they were now, that same countenance revealed nothing so much as a regimented hardness of situation. To the right of the road a metallic glacier of trash worked its way down a deep, smooth-sided gully toward the river, while to the left each of the village streets opened in the moment the Major passed it onto what seemed to Jim an identical sad vista. The white-frame houses were all built from the same story-and-a-half plan; an identical shed dormer peered from the roof of each house into the backyard of the house immediately downhill from it. Each house was marked near the ground by a splattered red stripe of mud, and each was tethered by a wire to one of the black power poles sprouting up out of the hillside. Coal smoke spun into the air from each chimney, where, in the light wind still blowing, it unraveled into a gray haze that gathered close to the rooftops and moved aimlessly off. The yards and streets were connected by capillaries of what looked like cow paths, down which, three times a day, a fresh shift of workers spilled toward the mill, followed, once the whistle blew, by the previous shift trudging home. Nobody was about in the cold afternoon, however, and only the cold, round headlights of old cars stared back at Jim.

Dennis Deane and Ellie Something lived on Leila Street. Colonel Allen, who had built the mill and the village in 1901, had named the town after himself and the streets after his children, but the street signs had been knocked down long ago, leaving the names to be passed along by word of mouth. Leila, Dennis Deane had directed Jim on a postcard, was the sixth street up from the river. He hadn't bothered to tell Jim the names of the other streets they would pass, and, as Mama slowed to turn off the main road onto Leila, Jim thought that all the streets could have been named Leila for the difference it made.

Mama stopped the Major in front of the eighth house, which differed from the seventh house and the ninth house in only the spindly-looking staircase that climbed the outside wall toward a small landing and a low doorway cut into the gable. Jim folded the quilt as best he could while Chrissie and Norma tiptoed out of the street toward the unevenly placed steppingstones that wandered through the yard toward the front steps. They carried the food basket between them. Norma sneaked a look at Jim and from behind her mitten whispered something to Chrissie, who giggled and whispered something back to Norma. Mama walked carefully around the rear of the car. Jim stepped onto the fender and hopped down.

"Did you get too cold, honey?" Mama asked. "At least the wind died down some."

"I'll live," Jim said. He handed Mama the quilt.

"I hope we didn't get it dirty," she said. "Let's at least refold it before we go in."

Jim turned his back to Chrissie and Norma, who seemed to be having a private and mutually satisfying conversation in the yard. "So when did those two get to be friends?" he asked.

"I don't know," Mama said, handing him back two corners of the quilt and briefly raising her eyes to glance at the girls. "I didn't really get the feeling that they had ever been enemies. Maybe being stuck in the car together did them both some good."

"What are they snickering about?"

"I think they like your hat."

Jim snatched Chrissie's cap off and shoved it in his coat pocket. "And why are you grinning?"

"Nothing, really. I'd just forgotten what it was like to be a girl. I had fun."

"Did y'all say anything about me?"

"Of course we did. You know you're the only thing we ever think about."

"Really?"

"Sure. With us it's Jim, Jim, Jim. Twenty-four hours a day."

"All right. All right," Jim said. "Did you like her?"

"This isn't the time, sweetheart," she sang softly.

"Did you?"

"I think she doesn't have an easy life."

"So?"

"But you do."

"What does that mean?"

"It means I don't really have anything against her personally."

"And?"

"You should be careful what you wish for."

"Are you slowpokes coming?" Norma called.

"There. That looks much better," Mama said. "I wish we could wrap it."

As they approached the house, a black-and-white

TONY EARLEY

hound stuck its head between two of the wooden front steps and snuffled loudly. Then it pulled its head back and disappeared into the shadows beneath the porch, followed seconds later by a moaning, theatrical howl. An unseen dog immediately across the street took up the call, followed by two farther down the hill. Soon, dogs were howling all over Allendale.

"Goodness," Mama said. "It sounds like the Blitz."

"This . . . is London," said Jim.

The front door opened and a short, round old woman appeared behind the screen. She put her hand on the latch but didn't open it.

"Y'all made the dog bark," she said.

Mama moved around Chrissie and Norma and spoke from the bottom of the steps. "Hello," she said. "I'm Elizabeth Glass, from Aliceville."

"Mrs. Tessnear."

"Good afternoon, Mrs. Tessnear. We're here to see Ellie and Dennis Deane."

"We don't like for them to have visitors."

Mama cocked her head slightly and touched her throat with her fingertips. "Oh. I'm sorry. I didn't know. Really?"

"Who is it, Ma?" a man's voice called from inside the house.

"It's for upstairs," Mrs. Tessnear said loudly over her shoulder.

"But they do live here?" Mama said. "Ellie and Dennis Deane."

"They do."

"And that staircase around the side of the house. Is that the way to where they stay?"

"The boys all work third shift," said Mrs. Tessnear. "They're in bed."

"What do they want, Ma?" called a second voice.

"I don't *know*. It's for up*stairs*."

"What does who want?" asked a third voice. "Is somebody here?"

"Up*stairs*. Up*stairs*, I said."

"Did Ma go upstairs?" somebody else called.

"Go to *sleep*," Mrs. Tessnear said. "All of you. Right now."

"My," said Mama. "How many boys do you have?"

"Seven."

"Are they all in the house?"

The old woman blinked suspiciously. "All except Ernest," she said. "Ernest ain't here."

"Ma? Why do they want to know about Ernest if they're going upstairs?"

"They didn't ask about Ernest."

"That staircase around the side of the house —" Mama said.

"What did you say about Ernest, Ma?"

"There ain't *nobody* said *nothing* about *Ernest*," Mrs. Tessnear almost yelled. "Go back to *sleep*."

"Ernest ain't here," a new voice said.

"Where'd he go?"

"I don't know. I just woke up and he was gone."

"Did he take the truck?"

"*Hush,*" said Mrs. Tessnear.

Jim heard someone hurrying down the outside stairway. Ellie Something peeked around the corner of the house before stepping onto the porch, her mouth agape. Jim immediately caught himself studying her breasts and just as quickly blushed. If she was showing, he couldn't tell. She crossed to the top of the steps and clapped her hands together underneath her chin. "Oh . . . my . . . goodness," she squealed. "Did all of you come to see *us?*" She ran down into the yard and violently hugged everyone, even Mama, whom she had never met, and Jim, who tried to get away. "Are those presents? Is that a *quilt?* And do I smell *chicken?* Oh, I can't believe how sweet you are to come all this way. Jim, are you cold? Your face is so red. Did you have to ride in the rumble seat?"

"The boys are in bed," Mrs. Tessnear said from the door.

"Yes, ma'am," Ellie Something said, turning her head to the side and speaking to the ground. "We know that."

"You know we don't like for you to have company."

"We have a right to have people come see us, Mrs. Tessnear. The boss man said so."

"I don't care what the boss man said. This was my house before you were even born."

"Well, we're sorry, but now we live here, too."

"I didn't have no say in that," Mrs. Tessnear said.

She stepped backward into the house and slammed the front door.

"You'd think she would be nice to me on a Sunday," Ellie Something said.

"Let's just go upstairs," said Mama.

Chrissie and Norma left the food basket on the bottom step for Jim to carry. He leaned over the railing so he could see around Mama and watched the girls as they walked up in front of him. Maybe Ellie Something's behind was a little bigger than it used to be, but Jim couldn't remember what it had looked like before. He didn't think he had ever looked at it. She had only been a freshman. Norma's waist and hips were curvier than Chrissie's, which somehow made him feel virtuous for choosing Chrissie over Norma. Not that choosing Chrissie had done him any good. Mama glanced back over her shoulder and he straightened up. On the landing, Ellie Something opened the door and extended her arm.

"Welcome to our home," she said.

Jim ducked into a long, unpainted room with a low bead-board ceiling whose pitch matched that of the roof. A cheap cookstove and a tiny sink dominated the room near the entrance. Beyond the stove, a narrow bed with an iron headboard lay partially hidden behind a chifforobe with a work shirt hanging from the door. The room was almost alarmingly hot. Dennis Deane, wearing an undershirt and owly horn-rim glasses, stood up from behind the table in the alcove underneath the dormer. The windows in the dormer overlooked the street, and Jim wondered why Dennis Deane hadn't come down to greet them.

"Well, I'll be," Dennis Deane said. "Look who's washed up on Leila Street."

"Oh, no," Ellie Something cried suddenly.

"What?" Dennis Deane said.

"This is just awful."

"What is? What's awful?"

"We only have two chairs, Dennis Deane. Where is everybody going to sit?"

"Chrissie and I will sit on the floor, won't we, Chrissie?" Norma said. "And so will Jim."

"And I can sit on the floor, too," Mama said. "I'm not as old as I seem. You and Dennis Deane take the chairs. This is your home."

"But why do *we* only have *two* chairs?" Ellie Something said. "Those awful Tessnears have probably got *eight* chairs down there. Maybe *nine*."

Dennis Deane looked a little frightened. He shrugged. "There are eight of 'em living down there. They gotta sit somewhere."

Ellie Something glared at Dennis Deane, then stomped her foot. Seconds later someone downstairs whacked the ceiling with a broom handle. She leaned over and stared angrily at the floor. "Ooh, you nasty old thing," she whispered.

"Ellie and Mrs. Tessnear get into it at least once a day," Dennis Deane said. "They're like two cats that way."

Ellie parked her fists on her hips. "Are you taking her side?" she asked.

"Oh, Lord, no, honey. Of course not."

"I'm just trying to make us a home here, Dennis Deane, and I don't have much to work with."

"I know you are, sweetheart, and I think you're doing a good job." He took the shirt down from the door of the chifforobe and rapidly began putting it on.

"Where are you going?"

"Me and Jim are gonna go for a walk. Wanna go for a walk, Jim?"

"Sure," Jim said. "I guess." He set the food basket on the floor.

"A walk?" Ellie Something said. "You're going for a walk? These people are our *guests*, Dennis Deane. They just got here and they brought us *presents*."

"Oh, I think they should definitely go for a walk," Mama said. "You see, our visit is kind of a surprise housewarming shower, and men would just get in the way."

"Absolutely," Chrissie said. "They should leave."

"The only reason we brought Jim," said Norma, "was because it was his car."

"And he didn't even drive it," Mama said.

"A *shower*?" Ellie Something said. "You're giving me a *shower*?" She covered her face with her hands and began to cry.

"Shh," Chrissie said, kissing Ellie Something on the hair and glaring dangerously at Dennis Deane.

Dennis Deane looked helplessly to Mama, who

winked at him and nodded toward the door. He stepped forward and placed his hand in the small of Ellie Something's back. "Hey, little stuff," he whispered. "Look at me."

"I don't want to look at you."

"Well, I can't say that I blame you there. I know I'm not the handsomest man in the world. But, if it makes you feel any better, I'm pretty sure I'm the handsomest man on Leila Street."

Jim saw Ellie Something's cheeks rise behind her hands in the direction of a small smile. She peeked at Dennis Deane over the tips of her fingers.

"We won't be gone long," he said.

"You promise?"

"I promise."

Ellie Something opened her hands and Dennis Deane leaned in and smooched her on the lips.

We're Married Now

$\mathcal{J}$IM AND Dennis Deane sat atop the large hump of granite protruding from the ground near the top of Mill Hill. Dennis Deane's glasses were pushed up on his forehead, and his hands covered his eyes. Jim thought that Dennis Deane might be crying, so he didn't look at him. He studied instead the names and dates and initials and hearts and curse words, some of them faded and ancient-looking, scratched on the cold gray skin of the rock. Because Jim didn't recognize any of the names or initials, and the dates held no significance, the curse words seemed to rise above the babble of their surroundings and fly in his face — which left him feeling vaguely picked on. It was like being laughed at by strangers for no discernible reason.

Below him, the houses of the village dropped toward the mill a terraced row at a time, trailing behind them backyards cluttered with coal piles and outhouses and roughly made chicken coops and recently turned garden spots; with fruit trees and beehives and small forests of tall poles blooming with purple martin houses made from painted gourds; with squat, black washtubs and clotheslines bobbing with gaunt families of dungarees and shirts and dresses and underwear. The houses didn't vary in shape, but somehow no two yards looked alike, as if another town had exploded nearby and the debris from the explosion had fallen randomly from the sky. Allendale from the front proclaimed its toughness with a single rigid face, but from the back it revealed instead a collection of tired private faces that Jim didn't think he was meant to see, particularly when a woman wearing little more than a slip appeared on one of the stoops and threw a pan of dishwater into the yard. Maybe that's why the rock he was sitting on cursed at him every time he glanced at it: he wasn't supposed to be here. He looked at his watch. He had been in Allendale less than half an hour and already wished he were somewhere else. He didn't know how Dennis Deane stood it.

Dennis Deane sniffed and drew his coat sleeve across his face and lowered his glasses onto his nose. "Ah, God, look at this place," he said.

"Do you know the names of the other streets?" Jim asked.

Dennis Deane closed his eyes and pointed down the hill. "Esmerelda, Honoria, Virginia, Eugenia, Cecily, Leila, Elspeth, and Garland."

"Garland?"

"The only boy. 'A nineteen sixteen graduate of Yale University, he loved his God and his country, and on the cruel battlefields of France willingly offered the frail vessel of his earthly body as a sacrifice for the propagation of liberty, July nineteen eighteen.'"

"Where did you read that?"

"There's a plaque beside the main gate. I walk by it every day."

"Does anybody still live in the big house?"

"Just Elspeth. The rest of 'em moved back to New Hampshire when the Colonel died."

Set at the end of an avenue of walnut trees near the high school, its first story obscured by overgrown box-woods, the big house had always looked haunted to Jim, although maybe its proximity to the ball field was what made it seem so scary.

"Have you ever seen her?"

"Who? Miss Allen? Nah. She only comes out at Christmas. Gives everybody a poke full of oranges. I'll get mine next year, I guess. I didn't get in the navy."

"You tried to enlist?"

"They said I didn't see good enough, not even with these handsome glasses."

"Where'd you get them?"

"An eye doctor comes to the mill every three months. Are you going to join up?"

"I already did," Jim said. "Did the mill pay?"

"Nah. They take it out of your check. Navy?"

"Army. I go in the day after my birthday. In June."

"I still know when your birthday is. What did your mama say?"

"I haven't told her yet."

"Boy," Dennis Deane said, "I wouldn't want to be there for that conversation."

"Me, neither," said Jim.

Jim hadn't wanted any part of the navy because there was nowhere to hide in the middle of the ocean. If the Japanese, or a U-boat, found your ship, you couldn't do a thing about it. Pearl Harbor had proved that. And even if you managed to get off your ship before it sank, you might still be thousands of miles from land. What were you supposed to do then? Besides, Bucky had been in the navy, and as far as Jim was concerned, that was strike three right there. He kept Bucky's letter from Pearl Harbor hidden in his underwear drawer. He didn't know what to do with it. Throwing it away seemed sacrilegious somehow, but keeping it never let Jim forget that Bucky, even though he was dead, had won in the end.

Jim had decided on the army during the train ride into New Carpenter the day he sneaked off to enlist. At least in the army there was a possibility you might get to fight in the woods, where Jim figured he would have a chance. The uncles said that country boys always made the best soldiers because they already knew how to hunt and shoot when they went in. Jim knew how to hunt and shoot. And if a squirrel couldn't see him, as good as their eyes were, then, how could a German? City boys, the uncles said, were always the first ones to get shot. The trick was to not stand next to one. Jim hoped that when his time came to fight, the battle would be in the woods.

"Who would you rather kill," Dennis Deane asked, "a German or a Jap?"

"I would just as soon not kill anybody, Dennis Deane."

"Well, you've got one bullet. And there's a kraut and a Jap running toward your foxhole. Who do you shoot?"

"The German."

"How come?"

"He's probably bigger than the Jap. I figure, shoot the big guy and fight the little guy."

"But what if the Jap was meaner than the German?"

"He would still be little."

"Man, if I could ever get out of this place, I'd love to go to the Philippines and kill me some Japs. I bet I could even shoot straight now. Have y'all been keeping up with it?"

"It sounds bad on the radio," Jim said, "but the uncles say that ol' MacArthur's going to be hard to whip."

"They're all screwed. Even ol' MacArthur."

Jim felt he should probably argue the point about MacArthur — the uncles would have — but deep down he agreed with it. He didn't see how anybody was going to stop the Japanese, so he let it go.

"Are you scared?" Dennis Deane asked.

"Some, I guess."

"Have you told Chrissie?"

"I doubt she would care," Jim said.

"You might be right about that. She and Ellie write letters back and forth, and apparently you did something to make Pocahontas awful mad."

"I told you not to call her that. What did she say I did?"

"I don't really know. Ellie won't say. She says girl stuff is private, and I'm inclined to agree with her. I know way more about girl stuff than anybody ought to."

"Do you like being married?"

Dennis Deane swallowed, then pushed his glasses up and covered his eyes.

"Are you crying?"

"Go to hell."

Jim looked at his watch again. Then he listened to it tick. He could feel the curse words on the rock trying to get his attention. He studied the purple martin houses down in the village to see if any birds came out of them. His butt felt frozen.

"I'm just tired, is all, Jim. Ellie cries all the time because she misses her mama, and her mama won't come see Ellie because Ellie got pregnant. *My* mama comes to see us all the time and starts crying as soon as she walks in the door. I don't really recommend knocking up a fourteen-year-old, Jim. It just causes trouble."

"I wasn't planning on it."

"The only real good thing about being married is that we get to do it whenever we want to."

"Really?" Jim said. "You can do it with a pregnant girl?"

"Oh, boy. Are you kidding me? That's all pregnant girls *want* to do. They're like daggum wildcats. Ellie likes to do it late at night when all the Tessnear boys are on third. It makes the bed squeak and drives the old woman crazy. Did you know your face was red?"

"Now you go to hell," Jim said.

"We'll take that trip together," said Dennis Deane.

"Well, we've got a good start."

"But first you've got to promise me you won't ever tell anybody I talked about Ellie like that. We're married now."

Jim still felt a little squeamish about the idea of doing it with a pregnant girl and couldn't imagine who he would tell, anyway. "I promise," he said. "Let's talk about something else."

"Tell me about Bucky's funeral. I heard there were two or three thousand people up there."

"There were more people up there than at the Christmas parade in New Carpenter, if you can believe that. Cars were backed up from the Bucklaws all the way down to Penn's house. They made Bucky out to be some kind of big war hero."

"Well, you know, Jim, Bucky is kind of a big war hero."

"He was on a ship and somebody blew it up," Jim said. "How does that make him a hero?"

Dennis Deane whistled and looked away. "Dag*gum,* Jim," he said.

Jim searched out and stared at the nearest curse word. He had it coming. "I know," he said. "I've got to do better. Please don't tell anybody I said that."

"I won't, but, boy, I can't believe you still hate him that much. I mean, he ain't coming home."

"He might as well be. He wrote me a letter right before he died and told me to stay away from Chrissie."

Dennis Deane laughed. "Some people ain't even nice when they're dead, are they? What time you got?"

"Ten 'til three."

"We need to go before long. I gotta be at work at four."

"What do you do in the mill?"

"I'm a sweeper."

"What does that mean?"

"It means I sweep. You see the third floor? That's what I sweep, every night, from one end to the other."

"Do you like it?"

"It's the worst job in the mill. The broom's four feet wide and it weighs a ton and it just kills my elbows. They only make dumbasses and people they want to run off do it."

"Which one are you?"

"I'm a dumbass. Ernest Tessnear is the one they're trying to run off."

"What did he do?"

"I'm not sure. He says they got tired of him not kissing people's butts. He used to be the guard in the gatehouse on first shift. Now he's a sweeper on *third* shift. And they made all his brothers work third, too. It looks like they're trying to run the whole crowd off. At least they gave me second."

"Why didn't they just fire Ernest?"

"They think they're teaching the rest of us a lesson. They're gonna wind up with a union in here if they ain't careful."

"Why does the old woman hate y'all so much?"

"They used to have the whole house. The boss man moved us in after they got mad at Ernest. We're on the waiting list to get our own house, but it might take a while."

"Why don't the Tessnears just quit?"

"I don't know. The whole gang tried joining the navy when they made Ernest a sweeper, but none of 'em could get in. They're all deaf from working in the mill. Me, I stick spit wads in my ears."

He stood up.

"Jim, do you remember all those times when we were in school and I acted stupid?"

"That would be hard to forget, Dennis Deane."

"Well, I just want you to know that I *knew* I was acting stupid. It doesn't really count as stupid when you know. Deep down, I'm actually pretty smart. I just tried to keep it a secret."

"Everybody suspects that, except maybe the teachers. I think you fooled them pretty good."

"I knew that one day I'd have to stop acting stupid and go to work and get married and all that stuff, but *damn*, Jim, I didn't figure it would happen this soon."

"It happens to everybody, Dennis Deane. It happens to me in June."

"Then we must have done something *wrong*. I ought to have some stupid time left. I ain't even grown up yet. Hey, can you hear that?"

The breeze had quieted for the moment, and in the lull Jim heard the faint hammering clack of the looms inside the mill. From a distance it sounded like cicadas, or banjos playing something fast, a rain shower coming across a cornfield, something other than what it was. He couldn't believe it was audible from so far away.

"Do you know what we're making down there?"

Jim shook his head.

"Khaki twill. Miles and miles of it. That's all we're running. Three shifts, seven days a week."

"For uniforms," Jim said.

"Yep." Dennis Deane hopped down off the rock.

"Hey, y'all might make the cloth for my uniform. Wouldn't that be something?"

"*'Y'all might make the cloth for* my *uniform,'*" Dennis Deane said in a whiny voice. "*'Wouldn't that be something?'*"

"What the hell's the matter with you all of a sudden?"

"There ain't nothing the matter with me," said Dennis Deane. "What the hell's the matter with you?"

March 14, 1942

New Carpenter, North Carolina
Dear Elizabeth,

Regarding your recent letter, I must take exception. Although I understand your position as the mother of an only son, I don't appreciate being taken to task for doing my duty. You should know me well enough to know that I would never certify any young man as unhealthy when he is as healthy as Jim is, no matter how long I've known his family. It's no easy thing approving any mother's son for military service, particularly when those sons are heading off to a war that's shaping up to be as bloody as this one appears it's going to be, and I don't take the responsibility lightly. Don't forget that I brought most of those boys into the world, Jim included! Please know that I will pray for him as I pray for all the others. Unfortunately, that's the best I can do. Be proud of Jim for wanting to serve his country. Don't blame me because you raised him properly!

Sincerely yours,
Theodore Burch Twitty, M.D.

p.s. It's been a while since I saw you last. Come on in when you're through being mad at me and we'll have a look at you.

"Heroes of Mathematics"

by
Norma Harris

MR. DUNLAP, *beloved faculty, family, and friends of the class of 1942, I stand before you tonight not as one who has arrived at a destination, but as one resting momentarily, as at an oasis, at the beginning of a much longer journey. Although we have on this day completed our long march through the difficult grades of elementary and high school, we are also fully aware that we have simultaneously arrived at a point of embarkation beyond which lie the disparate roads that will carry us to our respective destinies. For those of us whose destinies lead us away from our small, but beloved, home, we pray that those same roads will someday lead us back again, back to those of you who have selflessly loved and raised and taught us, equipping us for our journeys. We are also fully aware that, because of the great struggle in which our nation is now engaged, the days of travel ahead will be for many of us fraught with danger and hardship, and that all of us will be asked to make sacrifices greater than we think we can bear. [*DON'T LOOK AT J!*] Two of our number, Buster Burnette and Horace Gentine, have already heeded the call to arms, and others will no* doubt soon follow in their brave footsteps, and, lest we forget, those of us who remain behind will also be asked to make contributions no less important. We, the Aliceville School class of 1942, wish to assure you on this occasion that with God's help we are ready to do our respective duties, be they here or on some desolate foreign shore.

It seems like only yesterday that as a little girl I stood at the bottom of this very hill and watched this great hall of learning rise from the earth. At the time it seemed to me a miracle that such a gigantic building should suddenly appear in my tiny world. Today, however, armed with the education I received here, I look around this auditorium and think instead of the skill and knowledge necessary to make possible the construction that so dazzled my young eyes. From the architect who designed the building to the lowliest laborer, the individual abilities of each person involved were crucial to the building's successful completion, just as the individual abilities of each of us will prove crucial to our nation's efforts in the struggles ahead. It was the great Greek mathematician Pythagoras who said almost six hundred years before the birth of Christ that "all is number," meaning that the great truths of Creation can be reduced to mathematical absolutes. While Christ Himself proved Pythagoras's theory to be in error, I think we can now more accurately state that "much is number." I ask you now to gaze up at the majestic height of the ceiling above us and to note the great distance between its supporting walls. [GESTURE.] It seems impossible that the ceiling does not fall in upon us, yet it does not fall! We sit here tonight secure beneath it only because men who fully grasped that "much is number" used their considerable mathematical skills to build it in such a way that it would not fall. It was mathematicians such as Pythagoras and Euclid, the father of geometry, and Sir Isaac Newton, the inventor of calculus and discoverer of gravity, whose mathematical truths hold up the roof over our heads just as the democratic ideals of great leaders such as Washington and Jefferson and Lincoln support the enduring edifice of our republic. It was President Lincoln who said that "a house divided against itself cannot stand," and tonight we sit in this magnificent, undivided house of learning as citizens of an undivided nation, each of us one of a greater number committed to the preservation of freedom and liberty.

While the memories of the peaceful world in which we lived prior to December seventh remain vivid in our minds, I ask you to imagine another nation at peace, the ancient kingdom of Syracuse, on the isle of Sicily, in the year 213 B.C. In Syracuse at that time, there lived a mathematician and engineer named Archimedes. Archimedes was a peaceful man who was never happier than when solving a complicated equation or making a difficult proof. It was he who once leapt from his bath and ran naked through the streets of Syracuse shouting, "Eureka! I've got it!" when he finally figured out the solution to a particularly vexing problem — much to the surprise of his startled neighbors, I'm sure! It was also he who, while out for a stroll one day, gazed out to sea and spied the deadly warships of the Roman general Marcus Claudius Marcellus approaching Syracuse *under full sail! The Romans had come to invade and enslave the city in the name of the emperor! Though he was a peaceful man, Archimedes decided at that moment to use his mathematical skills to help defend his beloved city against the overwhelming might of the Roman invaders. First, using the laws of optics, he constructed great mirrors of bronze to reflect the blinding rays of the sun into the harbor and to set fire to the Roman ships that dared venture too close to shore. Later, after the Romans gained landfall, he invented great machines of war to defend the walls of the city against the relentless siege of the irrepressible legions. And when the Romans finally breached the walls and sacked the city, a legionnaire came upon Archimedes scratching one final problem into the sand with a stick, no doubt an equation he would use to invent yet another machine to help his countrymen. Archimedes didn't even look up from his work as the legionnaire drew his bloody sword and cut off the peaceful mathematician's head. It was Archimedes who said, "Give me a lever long enough and a place to stand and I will move the world." Though we did not ask for the responsibility, we, the class of 1942, have by circumstance and necessity been asked to take up the lever before us and move the world. You, beloved parents and teachers, have given us a secure foundation, a place on which to stand. Though we are but inexperienced youths, we understand that while we may not yet feel ready to move the world, move it we must, from the regions of darkness into which it has fallen, back into the light of freedom and peace. In generations to come, history will judge us by how we re-*

sponded when our nation called upon us. So years from now, when the day of judgment is at hand, let it be said that when the sails of our enemies appeared in our harbor, we set to work and directed the glorious rays of the sun back upon them! Though we long for peace, let us build great machines of war, and build them well, if that is what we must do.

Already we have lost one of our own to our dishonorable and inscrutable enemy, one who as a member of the class of 1941 sat in this very room just a year ago, filled with his own hopes and dreams for the future. No one here on that night, myself included, would have dared imagine that because of treachery already under way on the far side of the globe this young man in the prime of his life had but little more than half a year to live. Let it be known that the class of 1942 has voted to honor Arthur Bucklaw Jr. by leaving the seat he occupied last year vacant, and I now draw your attention to it. [PAUSE. GESTURE.] As we remember Bucky, I would like to close with the immortal words of Abraham Lincoln, who offered these sentiments during the dedication of the National Cemetery in Gettysburg, Pennsylvania, on November 19, 1863, following another dark moment in our nation's history. Though perhaps familiar, they have never been more apt: "It is rather for us to be here dedicated to the great task remaining before us — that from these honored dead we take increased devotion to that cause for which they gave the last full measure of devotion — that we here highly resolve that these dead shall not have died in vain, that this nation under God shall have a new birth of freedom, and that government of the people, by the people, for the people, shall not perish from the earth."

Thank you and may God in His infinite mercy bless us all.

Injun Joe

EARLY IN the evening Jim walked around the hotel and let himself in through the back gate. A dozen or so hens fussed over a yellow stripe of corn strewn from the porch, and he watched where he put his good shoes as he crossed the dirt yard. He still wore the black gown in which he had graduated — although he had left the cap at home — and he felt awkward and somber and ministerial and grown-up as he climbed the steps. When he peered through the screen he saw Chrissie seated at the enamel-topped table in the center of the dim kitchen, her hands crossed in front of her, her face tilted toward the small window above the stove. He watched her for as long as he dared before he tapped at the door. In the soft, slanted failing light she had seemed as beautiful as the Virgin Mary listening to the call of the Lord on a slick page in an old Bible, but as she turned toward him, her face lengthened and her hair dulled and dusky circles appeared beneath her eyes. The woman who stared back from the other side of the screen wasn't Chrissie at all, and the picture she occupied became almost too sad to contemplate.

"Come on in the house," Mrs. Steppe said.

"Thank you," said Jim. He still felt startled as he crossed the threshold and eased the door closed behind him.

"I figured you might be the first one to show up."

Jim didn't know what she meant by that, so he stood there and watched Mrs. Steppe watch him. He wished he had taken off the gown; and the necktie; and the shiny shoes. He wished he weren't holding a bottle of perfume wrapped in lilac-scented paper. He wished he were sitting on the porch at home with Mama and the uncles, watching people drive away from graduation. Uncle Coran or Uncle Al would say, "Good crowd this year," and Uncle Zeno would say, "Yep."

"I didn't mean anything by that," she said.

"No, ma'am."

"I just figured that you would come on by when you heard. You've always seemed to me like you'd be that kind of boy."

Jim wasn't sure what kind of boy that was, so he smiled and looked down at the package. He had been careful not to mash the bow.

"Y'all did hear about it over there, didn't you?"

"Yes, ma'am," he said. "We heard. I'm awfully sorry about Mr. Steppe."

"Yeah, well, Joe. It's been coming a long time, I guess, but it's nice of you to say that. Do you want to sit down a minute?" She placed her palms flat against the table and looked around the kitchen as if a new workday had sneaked up on her and had to be immediately subdued. "I've got half a pot of coffee left over from supper. Would you like a cup? It's still warm. We got an electric pot in the dining room, the hotel does."

Jim didn't particularly like coffee, but he was a high school graduate now, offering words of comfort to a woman whose husband had just died. By his reckoning this was the first purely adult situation he would handle on his own — an Uncle Zeno kind of situation — and coffee drinking seemed called for.

"Coffee sounds good about now," he said. "Thanks." He drew the chair at the end of the table and sat with his back to the door.

"How do you take it?"

Jim preferred that his coffee come with enough cream and sugar in it to make it stop tasting like coffee, but he answered, "Black." That's how he would have to drink it once he was a soldier. He pictured himself squatting around a campfire with other soldiers, drinking bitter black coffee from a tin cup. He hoped one of the other soldiers was his buddy. It would be good to have a buddy in the war. He wondered if it would be safe to sit around a campfire. Would the Germans see the smoke?

"Here we go," Mrs. Steppe said.

The coffee smelled better than he had imagined. The steam rising from the cup curled into the light falling through the window, and it seemed important to Jim that the steam climbing through the light be noticed, so he noticed it. Outside the window, the evening had begun to dim toward twilight, although the sun wasn't quite down. A chimney swift dove crazily across the small square of sky, and the bird's pale shadow blinked almost invisibly on the white tabletop and was gone. Jim noted that he saw both the bird and its shadow in the same instant, and that seemed important, too. He wrapped both hands around the cup and felt the heat creep up his forearms. The attendant beauty and sadness of the world suddenly seemed to him available for pondering in a way they never had before. He felt as though he had spent his life until this evening poised over an exam, waiting for the teacher to say, "Begin." Now he had begun. He took a slow sip of coffee but found that it tasted as bad as he had thought it would.

"You sure you don't want cream and sugar?" Mrs. Steppe asked. "I can get you some. It's no trouble."

"No. No, thank you," Jim said, placing the cup down on the saucer. Maybe the coffee would taste better once it cooled down a little. "This is good."

"I suppose I'll drink me a cup," Mrs. Steppe said. "It's not as hot in here as it was." When she returned to the table, she nodded toward the door standing slightly ajar across the room. "I guess you came by to see Chrissie, but she doesn't feel like receiving visitors this evening."

"No, ma'am. I understand," Jim said, eyeing the sliver of shadow visible through the crack in the doorway. "How's she doing?"

"Ah, about like you'd expect. That little girl sure loved her daddy. And he was good to her, in his way. I have to give him that, even now."

"And how are you doing?"

Mrs. Steppe's face dipped toward the tabletop. She seemed to be studying her hands. Some seconds passed before Jim noticed a tear flare in the light along her jawline and drop from the end of her chin.

"I'm so sorry," he said. "I didn't mean —"

She held up her palm and cut him off. She leaned down and dabbed the corners of her eyes with her apron.

"I'm fine," she said. "I just act a little stupid when people ask me how I am. I guess I'm not used to it. So, tell me, how was graduation?"

"It was nice," Jim said. "Norma gave a good speech." He instantly regretted mentioning Norma and hoped Chrissie hadn't heard. "It got hot in the auditorium before it was over, but we got through it."

Mrs. Steppe shook her head. "Joe, I swear to God," she said.

"Ma'am?"

"All that girl has ever wanted to do was be in school and be like everybody else and go to the dances and march down the aisle and get her diploma, and he figured out how to mess that up, too."

Jim sipped his coffee. It didn't taste any better.

"And I just can't believe that he was trying to come to her graduation," she said, her voice rising. "Did he think he could just march in big as life and sit down in the auditorium and nobody would notice him? Did he think he wouldn't get us in a world of trouble by pulling a stunt like that? Did he think we were going to up and go off with him, and him running from the law?" She picked up her coffee cup, then sat it back down in the saucer. "I give up," she said. "I don't know what he was thinking, and I don't guess I ever did."

Jim sneaked another look at the door.

"I think she's asleep," Mrs. Steppe said. "And she's heard it all before, anyway. I know I'm bad to get mad and wear Joe out. I don't guess I should, not in front of her, but I do. Most of the time I don't have anybody else to listen to it."

Jim began to sweat underneath his graduation gown. He wondered if he would spend the rest of his adult life not knowing what to say. If this was an exam, he wasn't doing very well at it.

"What did y'all hear about it over at your house?" Mrs. Steppe asked.

"We just heard that Mr. Steppe got killed in a car wreck. In South Carolina."

"In Chesnee," she said. "He was headed this way sure as the world. Were people talking about it up at the school?"

"Yes, ma'am," Jim said. "A little."

"I just bet they were."

"Nobody really knew anything, though. There wasn't much they could say."

"Did you know he was in a stolen car? Did y'all hear

that? Were people talking about that up at the school-house?"

"No, ma'am."

"I swear to God. That man. Stolen car. And it was a *Packard*, for goodness' sakes, like nobody on the road would notice an Indian driving a Packard."

"Were the police chasing him?"

"Not this time. He just ran off the road and crashed into a tree. They said he probably went to sleep. Ain't that something? Went to sleep and ruined somebody's Packard."

"I'm sorry."

"He never could do anything right."

Jim didn't know if he was supposed to affirm the remark or challenge it out of respect for the dead. So he sat very still.

"Maybe I can finally get me some sleep now, though. I figured all along he was going to come back this way. Every time I closed my eyes I dreamed he was looking in the window."

"Why were you afraid of him?" Jim asked before he thought. "Y'all were married."

Mrs. Steppe studied him, a slight frown of concentration and disapproval on her face. He had seen Chrissie look at him like that, and he was disappointed in himself that he apparently deserved it so often.

"You think married people don't get afraid of each other?" she asked.

Jim scratched at a small nick in his saucer. He had

gotten that one wrong for sure. "I don't know," he said. "I guess not. I haven't spent a lot of time around married people, I mean living with married people, so I can't say."

"Joe had a temper on him," Mrs. Steppe said.

Her tone and frown suggested that her answer contained everything Jim needed to know. He didn't know exactly what that was, of course, but maybe he could come back to it and figure it out later.

"Oh," he said.

"You know he robbed a bank."

"Yes, ma'am."

"You know how come?"

"No, ma'am."

She paused.

"There was this ranch for sale near where we lived in Oklahoma, but really what it was, was a dustbowl. Every time the wind blew, half of it wound up in Arkansas. Barns rotten, house falling in. You should've seen it. Anyway, one night Joe had a dream that the place had oil on it. He said he could see it underneath the ground, a whole lake of it, and he knew just where it was, and the dream was so vivid, he was convinced about it when he woke up. Absolutely convinced. I couldn't talk him down. He got like that sometimes. The only problem with his plan, of course, was that he didn't have any money to buy the ranch. Come to think of it, not having any money was always the problem with Joe's plans."

"So he robbed a bank?"

"That's what he came up with, yes. We didn't know none of this at the time, but he was going to rob a bank and buy that ranch and be the Cherokee oil king of Oklahoma. The bank he finally picked out was way out west somewhere, and the county it was in just had one bank and one cop. So who do you guess walked in while Joe was robbing that one bank?"

"That one cop?"

"The very one. Who naturally pulled out his gun and shot at Joe and hit the teller. Joe shot at the cop and managed to hit him in the foot. I know Joe wanted to kill him, but he couldn't even get that part right. Joe always did have bad luck with policemen."

"Then what happened?"

"The poor teller, he died, and the cop got crippled. Joe ran out the door, and we didn't hear from him again. That broke Chrissie's heart more than anything. Then, late one night, after they figured out it was Joe they were looking for, Chrissie came and woke me up, and there was a cross burning in our yard. It wasn't much of a cross, just a little dinky old thing, but still."

"A cross burning?" Jim said. "But you and Chrissie . . ."

"Joe ain't a white man," said Mrs. Steppe, "however much you might want him to be. And one white man was dead because of him, and another one was crippled. It didn't make any difference how white I was. And Chrissie was only *half* white. Soon as it got light, I took my egg money, and me and her hitched a ride into town and got on the train to come to North Carolina. We only had enough money that morning to get to Little Rock, but we started out."

"How did you finally make it all the way home?"

"I was able to get your uncle Zeno to wire us the rest."

Jim gulped his coffee and swallowed miserably. He had to be the worst adult on God's green earth. Uncle Zeno would have steered the conversation somewhere else long before Mrs. Steppe embarrassed herself. Mama would kill him if she ever found out he had asked such a dumb question.

"I just couldn't think of anybody else to help us," Mrs. Steppe went on. "I knew Daddy and Mama didn't have it, and I wouldn't ever ask the Bucklaws for anything if I could help it. You've seen how they think they own people. So, now we owe you instead. I haven't been able to pay it back yet, but I will. You can tell your uncle Zeno I said that if you want to."

"I'm sure he's not worried about it."

"He won't ever mention it to me, but I guarantee you he ain't forgot about it. The McBrides didn't get where they are by not worrying about their money."

Jim nodded. That was true enough.

"It was awfully kind of him, though. I wouldn't have blamed him if he'd said no."

"Does Chrissie know where it came from?"

"I'm afraid so," Mrs. Steppe said. "And I'm sorry about it. I know it would be better for her if she didn't know, but she does. The first time she laid eyes on you this year, she knew we owed your family money, and that ain't no way to start out in a new school. And I don't guess I should have told you just now. I don't know what I'm thinking anymore. I just can't stop talking."

"Can I ask you a question?"

Mrs. Steppe shook her head a little but said, "You might as well. I've told you everything else I know."

"Why did you marry Mr. Steppe?"

"Ah, I don't even know the answer to that one anymore. It seems like a thousand years ago. Because he was the prettiest man I'd ever seen, I guess, and because he could talk like nobody else I ever listened to. And he said he was going to live in California and grow orange trees and I liked the sound of that. California. Daddy had got his arm cut off and he owed people money because he couldn't work, and I'd hardly ever been off the mountain, and I'd never even rode on a train until I started going with Zeno, and then we only went to New Carpenter, and I thought, why not? Why not marry this handsome Indian and ride a train all the way to the Pacific Ocean, then get off and live there?

"At the time I was just so mad at Zeno for not joining the army. I stomped my foot and railed at him, but you know Zeno, he wouldn't budge once he made up his mind, so I broke it off with him. But that seems like a crazy thing to get mad about now, when you

think about it, because all them boys got killed for
nothing. Zeno was right about the whole thing. There
wasn't any reason for that war. Of course, you never
will know as much as you do when you're young, and
I knew everything there was to know. You didn't join
up because of Chrissie, did you?"

"Partly, I suppose."

She raised her coffee cup, then set it back down in
the saucer.

"I don't know that that seems like a good reason, to
be honest with you," she said. "There ain't never been
a little girl worth getting killed over, no matter how
pretty her hair is. And she never was impressed with
Bucky for being in the navy, not like the Bucklaws.
You'd of thought he was an admiral, the way they
talked."

"They probably would have got me in the draft,
anyway," Jim answered, his face hot. "Did Mr. Steppe
join the army because of you?"

"I suppose," she said. "I had pretty hair, too, you
know. He figured he could at least get one up on
Zeno, and he did. And I figured I could hurt Zeno's
feelings, and I did. Now, of course, Joe stayed in trouble the whole time for fighting with his officers — that
man never could stand taking orders from anybody — but he did get a medal for being brave. He
gave it to Chrissie a while back. She's got it squirreled
away somewhere."

"That medal must've made you proud."

"I didn't care much by the time everything was over with. Joe always was bad to be mad at somebody, but when we started going together, at least he had *resolve*. You believed him when he said he was going to do some big thing. But then when he came back from France, he was just mad."

"What was he mad at?"

Mrs. Steppe smiled sadly. "Oh, I don't know, just mad, I guess. Did you know Steppe wasn't his real name?"

"No, ma'am."

"His real name was Owl. Joe Owl. Steppe was the name of a missionary teacher he had at the Cherokee school who helped him get his scholarship at Raleigh. Of course, Joe, being Joe, never made it to Raleigh. He got off the train at some town down east and got in a fight with some old boys who didn't like a red Indian trying to eat in their train station. Then, when he got out of jail, most of what little money he had was gone from his wallet, and when he contacted the school, they'd canceled his scholarship. The cops had left him only enough to buy a train ticket, but not enough to make it all the way back to Dillsboro. That's how come him to get off the train here. This is where Joe's money ran all the way out."

"But that's not right, them taking his money," Jim said quietly. "Couldn't he take them to court or something?"

"That's not the way things work in the world."

"It ought to be."

"Do you think you'd still think so much of Chrissie if her name was Chrissie Owl?"

"Probably. I believe so."

"No offense, but you might and you might not. Joe's mother, Chrissie's grandmother, didn't even know how to speak English. All she spoke was Cherokee. What do you think of that? How would you like introducing somebody like that to your mama, prim as she is?"

"I don't know. I don't think it would matter."

"Well, it does matter. God knows Joe Steppe had a temper and a short fuse, and enough pride for ten Indians, but he also never got a fair shake, not once, besides that scholarship, in his whole life. If he'd been a white man, I wouldn't be a cook in a railroad hotel, I'll tell you that right now. We'd be *in* California."

"Yes, ma'am."

"You know how come she wears her hair like that, don't you?"

Jim shook his head.

"For Joe. He asked her to."

"I don't understand."

"It makes her look like an Indian, but she's white enough to pass. He said they were playing a joke on everybody, Indian and white, because nobody could tell what she was. It was their little secret."

"I still don't understand."

"I don't either," Mrs. Steppe said. "And I'm not sure Chrissie does. It was Joe's joke. How do you like that pretty hair of hers now?"

"I think it's beautiful," Jim said, blushing. "And I don't care who her daddy is."

"Was," Mrs. Steppe said. "Her daddy was Injun Joe Steppe and he robbed a bank and shot a policeman and wrapped somebody's Packard around a tree. That's who my girl's daddy was, and here we sit."

"Yes, ma'am."

"Now I got to figure out how to get him back to Cherokee. Chrissie would never forgive me if I left him in South Carolina, and I just know he would haunt me if I buried him around here."

At that moment someone slowly climbed the porch steps behind Jim. He noticed for the first time that he could no longer see Mrs. Steppe's face clearly. The square of sky in the window had darkened into a deep blue. The screen bumped gently against its frame, and Jim felt a whisper of evening air brush against his neck. Someone tapped at the door and he was afraid to turn around.

"Why, Zeno," Mrs. Steppe said. "Come on in and sit with us. I've been telling your nephew here my life story, and he's been nice enough to sit still while I do it."

Uncle Zeno removed his hat as he stepped inside. "Evening, Nancy." He nodded at Jim. "Doc."

"Hey," said Jim.

"Nancy," Uncle Zeno said, "we're awfully sorry over at our place about your loss. Please accept our condolences."

"Thank you, Zeno. Please tell your family I appreciate that. I truly do. Would you like some coffee? I've got about half a pot left over from supper. It's still warm. Jim don't like it much, but I think it tastes all right."

"Coffee sounds good about now."

Mrs. Steppe pushed through the swinging door into the dining room. Uncle Zeno hung his hat on the chair opposite Mrs. Steppe's coffee cup and sat down. He motioned with his index finger for Jim to lean closer.

"Go home," he whispered.

"They don't have any money to get Injun Joe back to Cherokee," Jim whispered back.

"I said, go home, Doc."

Mrs. Steppe backed through the door into the kitchen. "All right, then," she said. "Here we go. You still drink it black, don't you, Zeno?"

"The blacker the better."

Jim stood up. "Thank you for the coffee, Mrs. Steppe," he said.

"Why, don't run off."

"I need to get on home. Mama's probably wondering where I am."

"Do you want me to give Chrissie that present?"

Jim had forgotten about the package sitting beside his coffee cup. "Oh, yes, ma'am," he said. "It's not much. It's just for graduation. And please tell her how sorry I am about her daddy."

"I'll do that. Thank you for coming by."

From the porch Jim looked back through the screen.

The dark outlines of Mrs. Steppe and Uncle Zeno faced each other across the table. Neither seemed to have anything to say. When Jim turned toward home, he had trouble seeing the steps in front of him, and he had to feel his way into the yard.

BOOK IV

The Blue Star

The Sunny Side
of the Mountain

$\mathcal{J}$IM STOOD with the uncles in the front yard of Uncle Zeno's house. He wore a new gray suit and a sharp fedora and a fancy wristwatch, all birthday presents from the uncles the day before. Mama had given him the small leather suitcase, his initials stamped in gold between the latches, that now sat at his feet. He pushed up his sleeve and admired the watch — a proper soldier's watch, with luminous numbers and hands — without noticing what time it was. His old watch still worked fine, but the uncles had worried because it wasn't shockproof.

He glanced over his shoulder and studied the outline of the hat worn by his shadow. It looked strange to him no matter how he turned his head. Jim had never owned a real hat before, only baseball caps and hunting caps and the cowboy hat, red with white piping around the edge of the brim, he had favored when he was a boy. He felt like he was wearing a disguise, or someone else's clothes.

"You still look like a knothead," Uncle Zeno said.

"Sir?"

"It's a good-looking hat, but you still look like a knothead."

"A knothead wearing a hat," said Uncle Coran.

Jim wanted to respond in kind to the teasing but found that he could only swallow. He could not believe he was going away to places the uncles would not be. He didn't think he could find a hotel room that night in Charlotte without their help, much less find his way through a war.

Uncle Zeno patted him on the shoulder. "You look fair enough, Doc," he said. "All we ask is that you fill that suit all the way up."

Jim blinked. "Yes, sir. I'll try."

Uncle Al took the handkerchief out of his back pocket and blew his nose.

"Oh, Allie, don't start," Uncle Coran said.

"It's the hay fever," Uncle Al said. "And I ought to be able to blow my own daggum nose without everybody in town commenting on it."

"Boys," said Uncle Zeno.

Jim stared again at his watch so he wouldn't have to look at the uncles. This time he couldn't read the numbers. "What are we waiting for, anyway?" he asked.

"It's a surprise," said Uncle Coran.

"Just hold on," Uncle Zeno said. "Cissy will be along in a minute."

All four of them stared intently at the house. Mama finally raised one of the window shades in the parlor.

"Look. There she is," said Uncle Al, pointing. "There she is."

Mama climbed onto a chair and hung a white banner bordered by red on the nail Uncle Zeno had mysteriously hammered into the window frame that morning. In the center of the banner was a blue star. Jim couldn't believe his eyes. He didn't think he had done anything to deserve a blue star — he didn't even know if he would be inducted tomorrow afternoon or the morning after that — yet there it was, rocking gently back and forth in the window for everyone to see.

"Is that for me?" he asked.

"It's a service banner," said Uncle Zeno. "For our serviceman."

All three uncles pulled out their handkerchiefs and blew their noses.

"Oh, come on, y'all," Jim said. "Please don't do this to me."

"We've all got the hay fever," Uncle Zeno said. "And we need to get over it before Cissy gets out here."

Mama stepped down off the chair and pulled the shade without looking toward them. After a moment she pushed open the front door. Jim picked up his suitcase. It was time to go.

When Jim walked onto the platform at the depot with Mama and the uncles, a swarm of people enveloped him with noise and back slapping and teasing, for which he was grateful. Norma was there with her parents, and Dennis Deane had managed to borrow a car and scrounge enough gasoline to drive over with Ellie Something, and Pete Hunt glowered importantly up the track and studied his pocket watch and pretended nobody else was there, and even old Miss Brown and Mr. Dunlap had turned up to shake his hand.

Miss Brown wore a ridiculous hat covered all over with wax fruit. She placed her hands on Jim's cheeks and stared into his face. Her hands were surprisingly soft, and up close her eyes looked like those of a young person, which startled him.

"Remember the lessons of the *conquistadors*, young man," she said. "Do not let go of your helmet and sword, not even for a moment! Do not leave them lying about in Flanders Fields for someone else to find!"

"No, ma'am. I won't."

She leaned forward and kissed him soundly on both cheeks. "That is in the continental fashion," she said. "You will learn about it in France."

"Yes, ma'am," said Jim, wriggling loose. "Thank you."

Norma wrapped him in a fierce hug. Jim put his arms around her and closed his eyes and laid his cheek on top of her head. She would have been a good person to love, and he was sorry he didn't.

"You're my best friend," he whispered.

"Just come home," she whispered back.

Jim kissed her on the forehead and realized as he

did so that she had tilted her face toward him. They were acting in separate movies but had mistakenly wound up on the same screen. "Oh, Norma," he said, shaking his head. "I didn't mean —"

"It's okay, Jim," she said. "No use confusing everybody at this late date."

Ellie Something dove at him and he leaned forward at the waist so that their stomachs would not touch when they hugged. He looked at Norma over Ellie's shoulder.

"When I get back, you can teach me how to do calculus," he said.

"As if you would care."

"I'll write you," he said.

Ellie Something held him at arm's length and frowned. "Don't you make me name my baby after you," she said.

"I'll send my address to Elizabeth when I go to college," said Norma.

"What?" asked Jim.

"You heard me," said Ellie. "I'm naming my baby after Dennis Deane, and don't you forget it."

"That's me," Dennis Deane said.

"I don't think I could ever forget that," said Jim.

"My address in Greensboro," Norma said. "I'll give it to your mother when I know it."

"Unless it's a girl," said Ellie. "Then we're going to name her Thelma."

"Good," Jim said to Norma.

"Thelma," he said to Ellie.

"I guess I'll get out of your way, then," Norma said. "You've got all these other people to speak to."

"That hat makes you look like John Dillinger," Dennis Deane said.

"And we all know what happened to him," said Jim. He had always enjoyed that joke, but this time he felt the light leaking from his smile before he even finished the sentence.

"Oh, boy. I guess that's not too funny today, is it?" Dennis Deane said.

"No, but it'll be funny again the next time I see you."

"Just don't go to the movies in Chicago and you'll be all right."

"Did you hear that Dennis Deane got promoted?" Ellie Something asked. "He's a doffer now."

"That's great," Jim said. "What does a doffer do?"

Dennis Deane looked uneasily at the people crowding around them. "It's in the spinning room," he said. "I'll tell you about it next time."

"You got a deal."

"I'm not going to kiss you in the continental fashion, though."

"I'm glad about that."

"I'm not going to French-kiss you, either."

"*Dennis Deane*," said Ellie Something.

"I'm *especially* glad about that."

Pete Hunt shouldered in front of Dennis Deane. "Say, Jim," Pete said, "when you get to Europe, do you

think you could take some pictures of the train sta-
tions?"

Jim frowned at Pete. Not getting shot in Europe
seemed to him task enough. "I don't have a camera,"
he said.

"Well, I guess we need to be getting on back across
the river," said Dennis Deane, a little loudly, near
Pete's ear.

"Don't hurry. The train'll be here in a minute," Jim
said.

"Oh, forget I asked you to do that," said Pete. "I
don't know what I was thinking. I bet I could find a
book somewhere with pictures in it. I was just curious
about what they looked like."

"I'll see what I can do," Jim said.

Uncle Zeno tugged at his sleeve. "Excuse me, Jim,
sorry to interrupt, but I think you need to step into
the waiting room for a minute," he said.

Jim scanned the platform until he found Mama.
She looked okay. "Right now?" he asked.

"I think you probably better."

Jim stepped inside and closed the door. The shadows cast by his family and friends milled about indis-
tinctly on the floor around his feet, and the voices on
the platform withdrew to a great distance and ceased
having anything to do with him. Bright dust floated
upward in the light. No one was sitting on the single
row of seats facing the doorway, and the door to Pete's
office was closed. He thought he might be alone.

"Hello?" he called.

"Hello," said a small voice from the far corner.

Chrissie sat on the short bench atop the shoeshine stand. Jim didn't immediately recognize her because she had cut her hair. Now it fell just short of her shoulders, and she wore it parted on the side, held back by a single barrette. As Jim crossed the room toward her, she stood and looked down at him. Her eyes were puffy and bloodshot and the tip of her nose was bright red. He wanted to wrap his arms around her hips and hold his face against her belly.

"You cut your hair," he said.

Chrissie reached up and hesitantly touched the barrette.

"But I liked it the way it was."

She covered her face with her hands and sat back down.

"That's not what I meant to say," Jim said.

"It was, too."

"I don't know what I meant to say, but that wasn't it. I think your hair looks nice like that."

"You go to hell."

"But I do. It does."

"I don't know what I'm doing here," Chrissie cried. "I don't think I even like you."

Inside Jim's head two scraps of truth clapped into place simultaneously: one, she loved him — she wasn't happy about it, but she did — and she had come to tell him before he went off and got himself killed just the way Bucky had; two, he had made her life harder than it had to be from the day he had first noticed her getting off the school bus. Now it would be a long time before he could even start to make amends, if that day ever came.

"Can I sit down?" he asked.

Chrissie slid over and made room but she didn't look at him. Jim climbed up and eased onto the bench while she sobbed quietly into her hands. He placed his feet on the iron footrests and looked around the waiting room — at the empty chairs, the dented spittoons, the black stove, the green, soot-blackened walls, the print of Pikes Peak covered in snow, cut from some ancient calendar before he was even born. It wasn't, he realized, much of a place to leave from or, for that matter, come back to. In the whole world only a handful of people even knew about his going, and once his train left Aliceville, the strangers who heard it passing in the distance or waited on it at a crossing or glanced up as it shook their houses would not know that he was on it. And if that same train later carried his body by in the opposite direction, they would not know that, either.

"I don't even know what this old thing is doing in here," Jim said. "I don't think Aliceville has ever had a shoeshine man."

Chrissie didn't say anything.

"Back when I was a little kid, on rainy days I used to come in here and make believe that it was a stagecoach, and I would sit up here and pretend that I was driving it until Pete would run me off. I used to go all over the country."

"Could you take me somewhere?" Chrissie asked. She still hadn't looked at him.

"You would actually go somewhere with me?" he asked.

Chrissie drew a deep breath and nodded slowly.

Jim turned toward her and studied the back of her neck. He didn't think he had ever seen it before. It was lovely. He raised his hands, grabbing a set of reins. "Hold on, then," he said. "Yah! Get up!" He bounced up and down a few times and the bench creaked beneath him.

Chrissie lowered her hands and dabbed at her nose with the back of her wrist. Jim would have offered her his handkerchief, but it was already damp. She turned and looked at him seriously.

"Where are we going?" she asked.

"How about our place? Up Painter Creek. I think there's going to be a big stand of walnuts this year."

"I don't want to go back there."

"Why not?"

"Because you're going to leave me in that old house all by myself."

"But I would never do that."

"You're already about to."

That was true enough. He looked around quickly, a small panic flapping in his chest. "Then, how about that mountain over there?"

They gazed at Pikes Peak on the wall across the room.

"It looks cold," Chrissie said.

"We'll live on the sunny side," Jim said. "I'll build you a good house and I'll keep the woodpile tall and I'll buy you a new coat and I won't let you get cold ever again."

"Is that a promise?"

"It's a solemn promise."

"Do you think it will take us a long time to get there?"

"A while, I'm afraid. We might wear these horses out."

He could feel her staring at him, but he didn't dare look at her.

"Okay," she said finally. "Okay." She leaned toward Jim and rested her forehead on his shoulder. "Drive slow."

Jim slowly turned his face until his nose brushed her hair. He could smell the perfume he had given her for graduation. He closed his eyes.

"Then everything's settled?" he asked.

"Yes. Everything's settled."

"You'll wait for me?"

Chrissie sat upright, mashing Jim's nose in the process. "You should know that if I ever decide to love somebody again, I'm going to love them hard, and I'm going to love them for a long time."

"I could make do with that."

"Is that how you would love somebody if you decided you were going to love them?" she asked.

"Yes, ma'am," he said. "That's exactly how I would love them."

"You're really sure?"

"I'm really sure."

"Then, I've got something for you."

Chrissie reached into her skirt pocket and pulled out a tobacco tin, which she presented to Jim. He opened it and looked inside and shook out a long, thin braid of black hair, tied tightly on each end with red thread. Jim noticed that his hands were shaking, and he noticed that he had started to cry, but for the first time he also felt blooming inside his chest the certainty that he would make it home from the war. He would somehow make it back to Aliceville, and Chrissie would be waiting. Wherever he went after that, she would go with him. He reached up and took off his hat. He closed his eyes and leaned toward her, knowing as he did so that she would be leaning toward him.

The sound of the door jerking open startled him. "Jim!" Uncle Zeno cried. "Are you coming or not? The train's going to leave without you!"

"Oh, God," Jim said. "The train's going to leave." He hadn't even heard it arrive.

He clapped his hat on his head and leapt off the shoeshine stand and helped Chrissie down. He pulled her across the waiting room and out the door into an indecipherable swirl of shouting and crying and the dangerous, breathing proximity of the train. Some-

how he lost Chrissie's hand and found himself clutch-
ing instead the handle of his suitcase. People he
couldn't even see were pushing him toward the edge
of the platform, and he had the awful feeling that if
he got any closer to it, the train was going to eat him.
He looked around wildly because he had so much to
say to everyone that he should have said long before
now, but he didn't recognize a soul. Someone was
shouting his name in his ear and it was Mama and he
grabbed her and she weighed next to nothing. She
might have disappeared right then if he hadn't held
on to her. She kissed his face and both of his eyes over
and over and whispered in his ear, "Oh, Jim, I think
I'm going to die," and he squeezed her until he felt
her breath catch and whispered to her, "Nobody's going to die, Mama. I promise you. We're all going to
live for a long, long time." Then the uncles surrounded
him and kissed him unashamedly and he kissed them
back. Their beards were scratchy the way they had
been when he was little and their breaths smelled of
buttermilk and onions and he couldn't remember the
last time he had kissed them and he wished that he
had kissed them every single day of his life. One of
them said, "May the Lord bless and keep thee. May
His face shine upon thee," but he wasn't sure which
one it was. He had to tell them something important,
but Uncle Zeno said, "Don't worry. We'll see about
her while you're gone," before he even opened his
mouth. The conductor yelled, "All aboard!" from just
a few feet away and up the track a bell clanged evenly

and the engine snorted an impatient blast of steam. "Chrissie," he said, and suddenly her face was inches from his own and he kissed her and thought, *This is what my life tastes like,* and the knowledge was brand-new and it was the secret to everything and it thrilled him and he kissed her again and tried to remember it, but it wasn't enough. He would need to kiss her for years and years, and that wouldn't be enough, either. Behind him the conductor said, "Son, we gotta *go.* You've got to get on this *train,*" and the engine chuffed, and chuffed again, and the drive wheels screeched against the rails and the couplings clanked and the car lurched behind him and he said, "I love you, I love you," and let go and turned away and stepped off the platform onto the moving train.

ABOUT THE AUTHOR

Tony Earley is the author of *Jim the Boy, Here We Are in Paradise,* and *Somehow Form a Family.* He lives with his family in Nashville, Tennessee, where he is the Samuel Milton Fleming Associate Professor of English at Vanderbilt University.